CYBERWITCH

A MIDSUMMER NIGHT'S

featuring stories by

K. LASLIE
KOLIN GATES
JENNIFER LASLIE
BRITTANY WHITE
VICTORIA ESCOBAR
AVA LYNN WOOD

edited by

HEATHER MARIE ADKINS

A MIDSUMMER NIGHT'S SIDHE:

A CyberWitch Press Short Fiction Anthology

Anthology Copyright © 2016 | Heather Marie Adkins | CyberWitch Press LLC

Published by CyberWitch Press LLC

Louisville, KY

cyberwitchpress.com

cyberwitchpress@gmail.com

First edition, published October 2016

Individual copyrights retained by original authors: *The Witchwood* © Kolin Gates / *Fae Touched* © Heather Marie Adkins / *Finding Home* © Brittany White / *Tricky Wishes* © Victoria Escobar / *Ethereal* © K. Laslie / *Exiled* © Jennifer Laslie / *Burning Love* © Ava Lynn Wood

Cover Art by CyberWitch Press LLC

Stock Photo Credit: "Woman in the night" © Zulfiska5

Interior book design by CyberWitch Press LLC

STORIES INCLUDED IN
A Midsummer Night's Sidhe

INTRODUCTION

Sidhe: *noun* | \shee\ —

a: the fairy folk of Ireland in Gaelic folklore
b: a member of the sidhe: a fairy in Gaelic folklore

Faerie, my preferred spelling, derives from Old French and means *enchantment*. Fitting, because the land of fae and all its various imagined creatures have long dazzled the human race. Faery gained a foothold in early Europe, rooted in pre-Christian Celtic, English, and Germanic folklore. Today, the idea of the fae folk — or the *sidhe*, a term derived from Irish myth — encompasses many races, from fairies to pixies, elves to goblins, brownies and more.

With such a deep, forgotten history and a wide variety of races, faery allows for a certain creative freedom of expression in writing. In this anthology, affectionately titled for the great William Shakespeare's iconic classic "A Midsummer Night's Dream," seven authors have come together to delight you with tales of the wee folk.

Don your honorary wings. Acquire your preferred beverage. Curl into your favorite chair. And prepare to delve into the world of the sidhe.

Heather Marie Adkins
October 13, 2016

THE WITCHWOOD

KOLIN GATES

§

*T*hey entered the wood as twilight forced the sun from the sky.

"Lord Kraus," Bernhardt began. "Do you think they followed us?"

Wilhelm Kraus glanced at his man-at-arms, then flicked his reins. The trees were distracting him from the question that hung in the air. The men were nervous for battle. Wilhelm gave his horse a nudge to avoid an overlarge oak trunk.

"My lord?"

"What?" Wilhelm snapped.

"Are we pursued, do you think?" Geoff asked.

Wilhelm shook his head. His jaw ached from clenching his teeth, and he straightened in the saddle and opened his mouth wide to stretch the sore muscles. "No, man, look around you. Do you think Braunschweig's cravens would follow us here?"

His soldiers did as he suggested, and Wilhelm grinned as he saw a new fear bubbling to the surface. He hadn't recognized it at first, but as the sun sank lower and the warriors went deeper, Wilhelm knew where they were.

"The Witchwood? My God…"

"Aye, Hans," Wilhelm agreed. "The Witchwood. Couldn't have asked for a better time to visit, eh?"

"You jest, my lord," Bernhardt said woodenly.

"Of course." Wilhelm looked over and saw Bernhardt's sword was in his hand. "Nothing to it now. We either turn and use that," he said, jerking his chin at the bare steel. "Or we press on, superstitions be damned!"

None of the men replied, and Wilhelm saw them sink deeper into their saddles. He remained straight as a pillar, hoping to impart some backbone through example. Not that any of them were cowards. They were plenty fierce against a human enemy. But men that killed other men had a shocking propensity for superstition.

The Witchwood was ancient. Wilhelm felt it in his bones. It was the first time in twenty years that he'd set foot in the forsaken place. The last, and only, time he'd entered had been on a dare, and he'd been thirteen. He had run a quarter league deep from the Anhalt side of the border, turned, then run back the way he'd come.

Only it hadn't quite worked that way.

He'd run and run, for hours on end. The trees shifted and danced, reaching down with grasping branches. Sibilant sounds had hissed in the undergrowth, jerking him from his path to avoid whatever lurked unseen. Wilhelm shook the memories away.

"How much left until we reach Anhalt?"

Geoff answered Hans in a quivering voice. "Leagues…"

"The Witchwood isn't even a single league from end to end," Bernhardt scoffed. "Look at a map sometime, woolhead."

"You're one to speak, Bern! Why, you can barely — "

"Listen," Wilhelm interrupted.

The men fell silent. Wilhelm heard the groaning of leather, the chuff of horses, the crunch of early autumn loam. Under that, something else had caught his ear. A slithering. Something that *shifted* while it moved. Wilhelm narrowed his eyes, peering at the chaos of leaves and vines and dead foliage. He flicked his gaze among the men, nods answering his unspoken question.

They heard it, too.

Wilhelm drew his sword. Somewhere to the west, a warhorn bellowed. From the Braunschweig border. Wilhelm halted the party, holding up his hand for silence. Faint shouts and the clash of steel, the screaming of men giving battle. Wilhelm recognized those sounds, even through the thick trees.

"Let's move," he said, kicking his courser into a faster walk.

The trees were thick and dark, a permanent nightscape. A green canopy overhead made Wilhelm curse that it wasn't later in the season. His eyes had adjusted to the gloom, as much as they would, but he still felt the strain around the edges from peering into shadows. Ahead of them, something darted between fat trunks.

"What was that?"

Wilhelm held up a fist for silence. The column clanked to a stop behind him, all nine of the soldiers looking about with nervous faces. Wilhelm turned back to their path and —

All nine of the soldiers?

His heart pounded as he turned and met the eyes of his men. Geoff, Hans, Bernhardt, Adalbern, Erhard, Oswald —

"Where is Edgar?"

Oswald spun in his saddle, his horse stamping. Edgar's horse was standing right behind him, but Edgar was not in the saddle. Wilhelm yanked down on his reins, trying to keep his own mount under control. All of the animals were scared, their big, round eyes rolling around the forest. These were seasoned scouts, well-trained coursers that would run for leagues without tiring. Wilhelm had never seen them so afraid.

"Torches!"

Wilhelm freed his own torch from where it sat strapped against the tack. Hans was riding among the men, and Wilhelm saw the first burst of flame. It was like a beacon of hope, pressing back the shadows from the fell wood. Hans held the fire horn out, and Wilhelm stuffed his torch inside. He watched as Hans blew into the other end, then pulled his torch away as the pitch-soaked cloth caught alight.

Soon, they had a blazing sphere of light. The Witchwood seemed much less intimidating. The trees were just normal trees, only grown massive, in need of the woodcutter's axe. Then Wilhelm remembered why they'd lit the torches in the first place.

He spun his horse again, casting about for any sign of Edgar.

"Otto!"

"What?" Geoff shouted, but Wilhelm had already seen. They turned toward Otto's riderless horse, moving closer together instinctively.

"Christ! Where has he got to?"

"Don't blaspheme in this place, Bernhardt!" Wilhelm snapped. "Gather close to me."

The men moved their coursers into a tight pack, knees brushing and stirrups clacking.

"What should we do, my lord?"

"Take their horses. We must move. We'll come back for them later, but we must get this news back to Anhalt." Wilhelm looked around, hard eyes meeting with nods. "War is upon us."

"Aye," Geoff responded, chagrined at his question.

They all knew the stakes. Their information had to make it back to Anhalt, or entire towns might be decimated. An army had to be levied, supplies allocated. Braunschweig was on the move, ten divisions of soldiers, with an entire division of knights atop huge destriers. Even without their battle armor, those knights had been frightening to behold.

"Our families' lives depend on us, men."

Adalbern took the lead, spurring his chuffing mount deeper into the Witchwood. Wilhelm followed, and a brooding silence settled over the tight-packed soldiers. Wilhelm's thumb wore at the leather wrap near his longsword's hilt. A nervous habit, he'd rubbed the leather to a smooth shine.

Whatever had taken Edgar and Otto had been silent, and fast. His sword would probably be useless against it, but it felt good in his hand. He'd trained since he was a child, lost two of the fingers on his left hand, and survived to the ripe age of thirty-three. All a testament to his sword-skill. Most soldiers, even noblemen, didn't reach three decades.

Not in Wilhelm's Germany.

"What could have taken them like that?" Oswald whispered.

"Some kind of sorcery. Unholy, demon-fucking witches own this place. Maybe they needed food for their dogs," Geoff grumbled.

"How big is a demon cock, do you wager, Geoff?"

Snickers were suppressed under hands.

Wilhelm let them talk. He knew it would relieve the tension, and bravado was as much an antidote for fear as actual courage. As long as there were others around to see the charade. Wilhelm looked to either side, making sure all eight of his remaining men-at-arms were still with him. This time, he was pleased to see that they were.

It seemed that the halo of light they burned was keeping whatever evil had snatched Edgar and Otto at bay. Wilhelm swayed with his horse's motion, letting his posture slouch again. They worked their way eastward, frequently slowed by the massive trees and the lack of a path.

"Lord Kraus! Help!"

Wilhelm sat up in his saddle and cast about for the voice. It sounded like Otto.

"Help me!"

Otto burst from the tree cover and stumbled into the light. His face and arms were scratched and bleeding. He clutched a dagger in his hand, and he looked as if the hounds of hell were on his heels.

"Otto! What happened?"

"They took me — "

Otto was interrupted by a burst of motion from the same place where he'd left the shadowed trees. A creature, something, came flying at Otto. Wilhelm couldn't get a good look at it in the three seconds it took for the thing to emerge, grab the screaming man, and dash back into the trees.

"Get it!"

"After him!"

His men were moving now, the initial shock past. Otto had stabbed at the thing with his dagger, but it hadn't seemed to slow. Wilhelm kicked his courser into motion, moving into the forest. He thought they were going north, but without the stars above, it was hard to tell.

"Help!"

Otto's shout spurred them onward, through heavy tree cover and barbed bushes. Some of the horses were starting to rebel, jerking away from certain paths. The men struggled with them, and they were able to keep moving, but Wilhelm worried that they might lose the animals soon. He didn't want to be stuck on foot in this place, but atop a panicked, bucking courser was a worse place to be stuck.

A branch struck Wilhelm across the nose.

He grabbed at his face, blinded by pain. Around him, the shouts of his soldiers filled the air. His horse was still moving, and he still held his torch. When he was able to see again, he was glad that his horse had stayed with the others. The frantic dash through the wood had left them wide-eyed and out of breath.

"This is madness. We'll never find Otto this way," Wilhelm said. "Bernhardt, Oswald, get down and use your swords to clear a path."

Both of the men looked at each other, then at him for a long moment, but they dismounted. Adalbern took their reins and formed up with Wilhelm. The light behind him shifted oddly, and Wilhelm spun his horse.

A bulging green vine had wrapped itself around Geoff's mouth. Even though he struggled and thrashed, he couldn't be heard over the other noise. His horse was calm. The vines twisted around his upper arms, mailed chest, and stomach. Geoff's eyes were huge and pleading, and Wilhelm knew now how Edgar and Otto had disappeared in silence.

"Help Geoff," he yelled, moving toward him.

Erhard spun his horse and raised his torch. Geoff was still seated when the flames came near the vines. Wilhelm could sense the vines shrinking away from the fire. Just then, Geoff's dropped torch caught alight the loam under his horse. Wilhelm was still too far to help, and time slowed as he watched a horrifying series of events.

Something huge burst from the forest, barreling Erhard right out of his saddle. The vines around Geoff tightened and pulled, yanking him, twitching, into the air. Wilhelm saw blood leaking from his mouth. Geoff's horse, now free of whatever had ensorcelled it, panicked at the fire. The animal ran directly into the monstrous thing that was atop Erhard on the ground.

Wilhelm drew his sword.

The monster reared up, a mix of bear and tree, claws as long as a man's finger. It cleaved a huge wound into Geoff's courser's neck, and blood sprayed out in a fan. Wilhelm rode his horse abreast the beast, raising his sword high. Then he cut it backward, a hammer stroke. The weighted cavalry blade bit deep, and the monster screamed, then gurgled, then fell silent.

"Thank the Lord God in Heaven! Thank you, my lord," Erhard gushed.

Wilhelm dismounted, leaving his sword embedded in the monster's head. He held a hand out to Erhard. He helped the man to his feet, looking up to see if Geoff was alive. Geoff seized, blood pouring down ten feet, sizzling in the flames. Erhard gripped Wilhelm's hand fiercely.

"My... Lord — "

Erhard coughed blood into Wilhelm's face. Wilhelm hadn't seen it when he'd pulled the man to his feet, but now he did. Erhard's stomach had been ripped open, and he had left his entrails on the loam. Wilhelm went down on his knee, holding Erhard's shoulders to keep him from collapsing.

"My family..." Erhard choked out.

"They'll be looked after like they were my own. You are a good man, Erhard, and you will be welcomed into heaven," Wilhelm said, tears welling in his eyes. His voice was thick. "Our Father, which art in Heaven, Hallowed be thy Name."

The rest of his men joined them, and they spoke the prayer with Wilhelm. He let his tears fall. He had known these men since he was a youth. They had never been his peers, but they had been his friends and companions. Now Edgar and Otto had been taken, were likely dead, and Erhard and Geoff were dying in this evil place.

"Cut him down," Wilhelm said, holding Erhard through his last breath.

Adalbern rode up, able to get the tip of his sword through the vines holding Geoff aloft. He fell to the ground with a crunch. The fire had been extinguished by the wet ground and Geoff's blood. Wilhelm walked to the blackened puddle, but he knew Geoff was dead from the angle of his spine and head.

"Burn it," he murmured, staring at Geoff's corpse.

"My lord?" Bernhardt asked.

"Burn it!" Wilhelm shouted, spinning and facing the dark forest. "You hear me, witches? Forest monsters! Foul creatures, we will cleanse you with flame!"

Then, to the six men still standing, "Gather the bodies here. Did we bring an axe?"

"Two, my lord," Hans replied.

"Good. Start felling the smaller trees. You help him, Oswald. The rest of you, help me collect the horses and set up camp. Bernhardt, wrap Geoff and Erhard in their bedrolls. They won't be buried in this forsaken place."

Wilhelm and his men set to work.

§

SHE WOKE TO FLAMES licking up her legs.

A scream of pure horror rose from her throat. Then consciousness came slamming in, and she realized the fire was in the wood, not in her corporeal body.

"About time, Adeline."

Adeline looked up at her sisters, both awake and both staring down at her. She didn't bother snapping back. There were greater evils afoot, and petty insults seemed... petty.

"Help me, Almut," she said, reaching out.

Almut grasped her arm and pulled her free of her bed. Adelmoed stepped toward her and began freeing her legs. Adeline flinched as the small branches and vines were sheared away from her body. She felt blood leaking down from her thighs, coating her legs.

Adelmoed flicked her head toward the south, hair clattering around her shoulders. "Adeline, call your faeries. We need to know what's happening."

Adeline looked south and gasped. The source of the flames that had burned her body in her dreams were there, rising above the treetops. Black smoke covered the horizon, hiding the moon and stars. She did as her sister ordered, howling her summons across the Moonwood. Then she rounded on Adelmoed and leveled an accusatory finger.

"Where were your creatures? How did you allow this to happen?"

Almut pressed her arm down. "None of us know anything yet."

A plea to forestall the blame and infighting. Adeline was glad for Almut, their eternal peacekeeper. Without her, the two sisters would have torn each other apart and half the Moonwood with them.

"Men," Adelmoed growled. "It must be men."

Adeline nodded.

In the dancing inferno light, her fairies began arriving. The oldest and strongest of them surged forward, racing for her favor. They arrived in pairs and packs, landing all around the branches. She saw a few perish with spears through their backs, their killers smiling as their own position in the world went up a notch.

Always the opportunists.

"Go forth," Adeline ordered. "Find the source of the flames. Oorianthe, you alone will return to us." She paused as the other fairies' distanced themselves from Oorianthe, their lips curling in sneers. For her part, Oorianthe only made matters worse by giggling. "Unmolested! If any other comes in her place, those responsible will wish they'd heeded my words."

The fairies grumbled and averted their eyes.

"Go!" Adelmoed screamed, startling them into frantic motion. "Idiots."

"Stop it, sister," Almut snapped. "We need to raise a storm, and quickly, or there will be nothing left to fight over."

Adeline fixed her face into a neutral expression. Almut sighed and scrabbled up their heartwood. Adelmoed followed, leaving Adeline among the branches. She looked south again with a grimace, then skittered up the tree behind her sisters.

§

"MORE WOOD, HERE!"

Wilhelm pointed at a section of their ever-expanding fire that was flagging. Bernhardt rushed forward with an armload of thatch and threw it against the flames. Hans worked behind him, laying heavier logs into the circle. Wilhelm looked at their supplies, hoping they had enough to keep the fire ablaze.

He patrolled the inner boundary, listening to the furious cries of the forest creatures lurking outside. The bear-like monsters, with their shaggy, misshapen heads, seemed unable to combat the flames. Their bulging eyes reflected the fire, shining hatred at the men. Wilhelm could sense that his men were relieved at the reprieve.

As am I.

"Lord Kraus! Look out!"

Wilhelm glanced up just in time to avoid the huge stinger of a bulbous flying insect. The thing was the frontrunner of an entire army. Oswald drew his sword and began hacking the air as the creatures swarmed into their camp.

"Bernhardt! Hans! Keep the fire going!"

Wilhelm drew his own blade and braced himself, Adalbern at his side, as the first wave of the swarm approached. The purplish creatures buzzed violently as they dove for the warriors' heads. Wilhelm hacked inexpertly, wishing they'd brought helmets. Mail under surcoats might protect their torsos from the lancing stingers, but their heads were woefully unprepared for this new threat.

His blade bit deep into one of the things, and it gushed forth black liquid. It screamed over the crackling of the flames and buzz of wings. Wilhelm's eyes widened at the human-like sound, but he slammed his sword into the ground and kicked the thing away. Then, he was forced to duck as he sensed something speeding toward his head.

He looked up in time to see one of the insects, as big as a melon, slam into Adalbern's side. The man screamed, but his fist knocked the monster down and his boot stomped its guts into the ground. Wilhelm closed his eyes to avoid the splash, then he scrambled up and began laying into the evil things, dodging their finger-sized stingers.

After what felt like hours, he had a pile of corpses around him, and a few scrapes and stings in return. One particularly deep sting had taken him in the upper arm, making his left arm pulse with pain. At least the limb still responded to his commands.

Adalbern was down, spitting and choking.

Wilhelm rushed to his side and fell to his knees. A stinger had broken off in the man's neck, a thick black hole where it penetrated Adalbern's throat. Blood oozed around the wound, and Wilhelm knew that if he were to remove the thing, Adalbern would die in minutes.

"Lord Kraus — " Adalbern was interrupted by a fit of coughing.

Wilhelm held his hand over the man's injury, trying to keep the stinger from going deeper.

"Burn my body..."

"Are you sure, Adalbern?"

"I won't be damned — " A gurgle rose with his words, and Wilhelm saw blood on the soldier's teeth. "I'd rather not see heaven than be... here."

Wilhelm nodded, then began praying.

Adalbern yanked the foul stinger from his throat, blood and black fluid welling up from the hole. Wilhelm prayed through his tears. Adalbern held his gaze until Wilhelm saw the light fade from his eyes. He closed them, and stood, Adalbern's body limp in his arms. His left arm was screaming, but Wilhelm wouldn't leave him where he lay.

"My lord," Oswald said, rushing to help him. "Something..."

A crack of lightning tore across the sky, followed quickly by a blast of thunder. Wilhelm looked up, his mouth hanging open. He fell to his knees as the skies opened in a torrent of rain. A bitter slurry of ash and water washed into his mouth, and he screamed impotent fury at the heavens.

§

OORIANTHE RETURNED WITH A fluttering buzz of little wings.

Adeline sensed her, but knew she would wait to give her report until they finished. She and her sisters were anchored to the upper branches of the tree by their lower limbs. Almut's arms were raised to the sky, her will drawing dark, heavy clouds from all around. Adeline chanted with Adelmoed, lending her power to her sister's expertise.

The Bloodtree surged beneath them, thrusting its limbs, and Adeline with them, high into the air. From their perch, she could see the devastation wrought by the humans. Adeline blocked out the hurt and smiled when a snapping bolt of lightning tore across the sky, followed by a massive thunderclap.

Then, the sky opened in a healing deluge.

Adeline laughed frantically, her face raised to the cold raindrops. She felt the pain in the Moonwood slowly fading as the water began to smother the raging flames. Oorianthe buzzed at her shoulder, excited and triumphant.

"My beautiful little friend, what news?" Adeline asked.

Oorianthe shifted her curvaceous torso and displayed her spear proudly.

"We've killed two of the humans, and injured the rest!" the fairy squeaked.

"How many remain?" Adelmoed said, her tone sharp.

"Five, and horses."

"Did you see a leader?" Adeline asked.

"Yes! A hulking brute, more adept with his weapon than the rest. We stung him with spears but he resisted, killing many." Adeline stroked Oorianthe's shoulder, comforting the distraught fairy. "They call him *Lord Kraus*," she said, the foreign words harsh on Adeline's ears.

"A lord..." Almut murmured. "Could it be?"

"It's been decades," Adelmoed scoffed.

"Open your senses," Adeline said. "It *feels* like him."

Adelmoed clattered her annoyance, but Almut silenced her.

"I think you're right, Adeline. I feel it too!"

"*Feelings*," Adelmoed snarled. "I'm going to go slay the invaders. Those are my feelings!"

"Yes," Adeline began, her smile growing wide and bright. "Yes, kill them! Then we'll take him, and our vision can finally be realized."

Almut touched her arm and shared a warm smile.

Then they followed Adelmoed's disappearing form. Adeline savored the feeling of being alive, her limbs grazing branches and leaves. She hadn't been fully awake in so long. Every time she was, she realized what she was missing in her long sleeps, but also what she was preserving. She made a promise to herself to wake more frequently.

Rain pelted down through the canopy, striking her back and making little explosions in the loam before her. Adeline reveled in the run, loping through the wet Moonwood, dodging trees, climbing over fecund corpses. She felt her fairies in the distance, fighting and dying. Oorianthe flew at her shoulder, spear twitching.

"Take the dead ones," Almut shouted. "Adelmoed's creatures will shield us. These humans have a strange attachment to their corporeal bodies."

"Yes! We'll bait him," Adeline hissed.

"They'll serve to regrow what they've destroyed."

Adelmoed still hadn't agreed to their plan, something which was increasingly bothering Adeline. If she slew the lord, they might never have another opportunity like this. They'd almost had him decades ago, when he'd first trespassed in the Moonwood.

"Adelmoed," Adeline panted, winded from the run. "You must *not* kill the lord. If he truly is one of the Knightlords, we *must* use this opportunity!"

Adelmoed didn't respond at first, and Almut looked over, distraught.

"If you believe that your ridiculous scheme will work," Adelmoed clattered. "Then I suppose I can suffer the human." Adeline and Almut thanked her, but she wasn't done. "For a time! If he grows too intolerable, then I'll end him."

They agreed quickly. While Almut might be the peacekeeper, she and Adeline both knew who the most physically powerful was. They had enough to deal with without fighting among themselves.

§

WILHELM SPUN AWAY FROM his opponent just in time to see three spider-like monstrosities skitter into their camp. The horses that had not slipped their ties shifted away from the creatures, stamping and chuffing. He squinted through the slicing rain and his eyes widened when he saw what they had come for.

"To the camp!"

Wilhelm's shout brought the heads of his men around, and an explosion of curses.

The large, slender abominations each had a corpse in four of their arms, while their other limbs propelled them away from the camp. Behind him, Wilhelm heard his men, and their attackers, giving chase. He leaped into a courser's saddle and cut the horse's tie. Blood made the reins slick in his hands until he could get them wrapped around his wrists.

Wilhelm looked back for a moment, long enough to see the desperate battle raging at their camp. The forest monsters appeared to be winning, their large paws swiping at men and horses. He turned back to the burnt ground his horse was speeding over.

I must stop them.

That's what he told himself.

He knew though, as his horse passed the boundary of their extinguished fire, that he had already lost the spiders. He also knew that he wouldn't stop his horse, and if his horse foundered, that he would keep moving until he was free of the Witchwood.

"God, forgive my weakness," Wilhelm mumbled.

The trees loomed around him, sheltering him from the downpour. Forest noises overtook the sounds of violence. Wilhelm found himself glancing about, expecting something to leap from cover and maul him. Nothing did, and soon enough, the normalcy of it all began to creep up on him. He slumped in the saddle, exhaustion and relief forcing his eyes closed.

Wilhelm jerked awake, eyes wide.

Nothing there.

He vowed not to drift off again. Wilhelm studied the trees and frowned. Hadn't they passed this section of the wood before? He saw the fallen trunk that they'd had to circumnavigate, right next to the big oak with the creeper vines. His horse moved past, but Wilhelm's gaze remained behind.

Were they walking in circles?

With the night, the clouds and smoke, and the heavy tree cover, it was hard enough to see. The only illumination came from green lichens growing at the bases of some of the plants. That, and the occasional rip of lightning. Then the forest would light up for a moment and Wilhelm's vision would be ruined for ten times that after.

"This is madness," he grumbled.

There was a kind of natural lean-to up ahead. Two birch trees had fallen near an oak, which deposited leaves and detritus atop. Crude, but it would do until Wilhelm could see properly. He dismounted and took both saddlebags from the tack but left the courser saddled. The bridle was loosened, and the bit removed, but Wilhelm left the rest in place.

"Stay ready, friend," Wilhelm said.

The horse stared at him, and snorted.

Wilhelm sat heavily, digging through the bags for food. He didn't have any water, and his throat was desperately dry. An apple provided some moisture, and Wilhelm began to feel better huddled in his shelter. The apple tasted off, coppery, but Wilhelm was hungry.

He threw the core as far as he could when he was done, cursing. Then he drew his sword across his lap and hunched his shoulders. He wouldn't sleep long, just enough to get some energy, and some light.

§

"HE'S RESTING," ADELINE PURRED.

Almut rubbed her hands together. "We have him this time, sisters!"

Adelmoed scoffed and kept working.

Adeline's portal collapsed, her view of Lord Kraus dissipating.

The clearing they stood in was a scar on the Moonwood. Men always left scars, but these had left the most hideous the wood had seen in centuries. They would help heal them.

Adeline tapped the soil around the nearest corpse's shoulders.

This was the last of them. The rest had been planted around the burnt clearing. Their lolling heads jutted from the landscape. Adeline thought she sensed regret in their expressions, but she had never been good at reading humans.

It was a nice thought, all the same.

"We need to prepare."

Almut nodded and Adelmoed shrugged.

"Do you have everything you need?" Adelmoed asked.

Adeline removed a vial from one of her pouches in response. The dark liquid inside twinkled in a sudden flash of lightning. Adelmoed gestured impatiently. Almut rubbed her hands together in anticipation.

The stopper fell among the ashes and Adeline upended the contents of the vial into her mouth. It was disgusting; centuries-old spell remnants and human blood made her cringe. Adeline waited, nervous, hoping that the spell she and Almut had concocted years ago would still work. Then she felt the change begin.

Adeline coughed and choked as her limbs snapped together. She felt them fusing into two arms and two legs. Her torso crackled as a spine grew inside of her body. Skin crumbled away and flaked onto the ground she knelt upon. Her head elongated, and her bones broke, pushed through her skin, and reformed in a different configuration. Hair burst from her new scalp and fell until it swung in the ashes on either side of her head. Adeline's eyes changed, and she panicked suddenly when she could no longer see properly.

She jerked her head up and cast about, finding the forest set in some eerie non-light. It was dark, almost menacing. Was this how humans viewed her beautiful home? She turned to her sisters.

Almut's eyes were wide, and her teeth clattered with anticipation. Adelmoed's eyes were wide with horror, her gaze flitting over Adeline's transformed body with disgust.

"It worked!"

Adeline cringed at what came out of her mouth. Never had she heard the language of her ancestors so garbled and unintelligible. Human mouths were not meant to form real words. She tried again in the human tongue, in which both of her sisters were fluent.

"It worked," she croaked, the human words easier to form, but odd and foreign.

"Yes," Adelmoed chittered, her revulsion clear.

"Yes," Almut said. "Now, to gather the prey..."

§

WILHELM WAS RUNNING.

He looked over his shoulder at the mold-covered stone walls. He hadn't seen it yet, but he knew something was back there, something evil. It had been a while since he came to Castle Ballenstedt's cellar. The place seemed more like a dungeon than he remembered.

Ahead, there was an intersection. Wilhelm turned left.

"Wait," a woman said.

He turned and saw Elise, his wife, standing in the passage to the right. She faced him, wearing a nightgown, her long hair flowing over her shoulders. Wilhelm turned and rushed toward her, but just as his hand was about to catch hold of hers, she flew backward.

Elise screamed as something dragged her down the hall at an

unnatural speed. Wilhelm gave chase. Elise disappeared from view in the gloom. Wilhelm tried to push himself to faster speed. A few slamming heartbeats later, her screams had faded as well.

Wilhelm punched the wall, then screamed and sank to his knees. His knuckles felt broken. He cradled the hand to his chest, listening to a new sound. It reminded him of the time he had visited the beehives at the local meadery.

A low buzz, growing deeper and louder.

The first thing he noticed upon waking, was that he was lying on his left hand. It throbbed beneath him. Wilhelm opened his eyes and saw his sword on the ground. When his horse began screaming, he grabbed the weapon and stood, slamming his head against one of the fallen birch trunks.

For a moment, he couldn't make sense of what he was seeing in his blurred vision. His horse appeared to be thrashing at nothing, kicking and bucking. Then the animal turned, and Wilhelm saw what was on his back. Stabbing and tearing, the bloated flying insects that had attacked the camp were swarming all over the courser. Wilhelm saw bone in a few places. When he cut the tie, the horse flew away into the trees, his attackers clinging.

Then Wilhelm saw something that made his mouth go slack.

A beautiful woman stood where the horse had been. She looked confused, naked, staring around at the looming forest. Wilhelm's heart leaped into his throat at the thought of an innocent woman trapped in this hellish place. He ran forward.

The woman recoiled from him. Wilhelm frowned, then looked down at himself. His sword hung limp in his hand and he sheathed it quickly. Then he saw the grime, dried gore and rips that marred his clothing. He looked up, hoping his expression would calm her.

"Lady," he said, urgently. "It's not safe here. Let me help you."

"Where is this?" she asked.

Her voice was thick and the words came with effort. Wilhelm thought she must be foreign, from her words as much as the way she said them.

"Here." He extended his hand. "I've got a cloak."

"What need have I for a cloak?"

Wilhelm squinted and shrugged. "My lady, you're naked."

"Oh," she said, glancing down.

Then she took his hand and smiled, a tiny wisp of a smile.

She was young, maybe in her twenties, and slight. Wilhelm was reminded of Elise in their youth. She had the same black hair, the same curve of the waist. He blushed when he found himself staring at her breasts, which were just about right as well. The two women could be sisters.

Wilhelm dug around his shelter until he located his cloak, thrown aside while he slept. The woman took it, but seemed unfamiliar with the clasp. Wilhelm stepped close to her and draped the heavy cloth over her shoulders, his fingers lingering on her neck. She turned, mouth open, and stared up at him.

"What is your name?" he breathed.

"Adeline."

"I am Wilhelm Kraus," he said.

She nodded, and Wilhelm thought he saw recognition in her eyes. He shook the thought off. He had never seen this woman in his life.

"Are you hungry?"

She nodded and let him lead her into his shelter.

Wilhelm sat and spread out the contents of the saddlebag. He held out an apple to the woman, who recoiled from the fruit. He had heard that the color of fruit could mean poison to different cultures, so he set it aside. Adeline stared at him, not moving or speaking. Wilhelm tried some pork next.

"What is this?" she asked.

"Pork," he replied. When she just frowned, he went on. "Pig meat, cured with salt and sugar and smoke."

"Ah," Adeline said.

Wilhelm was about to attempt another explanation when she bit into the meat. Her incisors tore away a piece, and she smiled while she chewed.

"I don't have any water," Wilhelm said.

Something moved outside of their shelter.

Wilhelm stood, hand on sword hilt. Adeline stood as well and held up a palm. He watched her move out of the shelter in a crouch and followed. When there was no apparent threat, Wilhelm relaxed. Adeline bent down, then stood and approached him carefully.

"Here," she said, extending a gourd of some sort.

Wilhelm took it from her and saw that it had been broken open and filled with rain water. He sniffed the liquid, not fully trusting anything of the forest to be safe to consume. Adeline frowned at him and laid her hand upon his, helping him raise the gourd. Wilhelm's thirst finally overcame his caution, and he drank deeply.

The water exploded on his tongue, tasting fresh and clean.

Adeline smiled and took another bite of the meat. Wilhelm smiled back, losing himself for a moment in her dark eyes. Her lashes were thick, and she had a natural shadow on her upper lids that brought out the bright intelligence in her gaze. Behind her, Wilhelm saw something rise up. Adeline turned and screamed.

A brown monstrosity filled the space between two trees. One of the abominations that had attacked the camp. Up close, Wilhelm was surprised at the sheer size of the monster. Its long legs put the main portion of its body at almost chest height on him. He jumped forward and pushed Adeline behind him, then fumbled with his sword.

The spider was faster.

It lashed out, snapping Wilhelm up in thorny arms. He flailed, trying to break its iron grip. The thing chittered as it dragged him to its mouth. Dark ooze coated its mandibles, and Wilhelm punched out, trying to avoid them. Instead, the spider moved with him and clamped down on his forearm. Wilhelm screamed in terror and watched as the long fangs sank deep. He shuddered at the thought of the poison coursing through his veins.

Then he couldn't move.

His head lolled, and he saw Adeline in the grips of a second monster. He tried to call out, but his throat was tight and no words came. Then they started moving. The spider held him almost gently, speeding around trees and over debris. Soon, they came upon the campsite. The dead eyes of his men glared up at him from where they had been buried in the charred ground.

Panic raced through him, but he was powerless to resist his captor. The abominations screeched at each other for a moment as Wilhelm's eyes flicked around, the only part of his body still under his command. The camp had been torn apart by the forest creatures. Tents shredded, their carefully piled wood scattered all over the clearing.

He looked at Adeline, dangling upside down, and met her fearful glance with as much courage as he could muster. Without being able to move his face, he couldn't tell if she was reassured. Then they set off again, and he lost her in the swaying motion.

§

ADELINE WAS ELATED. RIDING in Almut's gentle grasp, she struggled not to smile.

For now, she had to keep pretending. Wilhelm had been fooled completely up to this point, so far as she could tell. The ritual would fail if he understood what she was.

"Faster," she purred quietly, urging Almut on.

§

WILHELM MOVED HIS FINGERS. It was enough.

Knowing that he would soon be able to fight back against his captor was heartening. The spider had been traveling for a while, following its companion, who carried Adeline. He had spent the first few minutes frantic, trying to think of what they might be planning. Eventually, Wilhelm accepted that it didn't matter and started thinking about how to fight back.

Now the creatures slowed.

Ahead, a small clearing was lit by fledgling rays of sunlight. The morning rays filtered through the trees, illuminating the tableau in fae light. The spider dropped him onto his back, and Wilhelm ogled up at the tallest tree he had ever seen. It dripped menace, huge and challenging; red leaves draped along branches that looked to brush the very heavens. Wilhelm felt like the tree was alive and conscious, and very aware of his presence.

He groaned and tried to move as he felt the spider's claws tugging at his clothing. Only his fingers moved, and Wilhelm was helpless against this new violation. The spider turned him over, clicking and whining, and finished stripping him. Then he was rudely flopped onto his back. Above him, the insectile face of his captor looked down impassively. There was no way to read any human emotion in its expression. Then it was gone.

All around him, Wilhelm felt a surge of energy. The tree swelled and swayed, seeming to grow even wider and more menacing. He was able to move his head again, and saw the abominations doing a weird dance in the clearing. They skipped from place to place, stopping to alight for a moment here or there. Wilhelm couldn't see exactly what they were doing from his angle.

He started at a soft touch on his chest.

Adeline was there, her hair falling in waves against his body. He couldn't move his arms or legs fully yet, but his fingers and head were responding. Her hand gripped his fiercely, and Wilhelm looked up at her with a wan smile.

"What will they do with us?" she asked.

"We'll fight them," he growled, knowing he must sound ridiculous.

"Wilhelm, they are…"

Adeline trailed off, and Wilhelm saw why as she moved to afford him a view.

One of the spiders was throwing half of a horse into a gaping maw that appeared on the tree. The tree's mouth crashed down. It chewed with a crunching, snapping sound. Then the tree split again, revealing a red hole that dripped gore.

The other spider threw in an unidentifiable corpse. A shaft of light illuminated the spider, and Wilhelm saw that it only resembled an arachnid. It had six long legs, and two shorter limbs higher up that he thought of as arms. The torso curved, making the upper half stand aloft of the body. The whole creature appeared to be made of hard brown bark, or some kind of carapace. It finished its task and skittered past him, green eyes focused on him as it passed.

"Unholy," Wilhelm breathed, shuddering.

Adeline's hand left his chest in a rush.

"Wilhelm!" she screamed.

Wilhelm sat sluggishly, seeing the woman being dragged away by her feet. The creature that gripped her moved away slowly, its eyes on Wilhelm, not its prey. The woman's dark hair streamed behind her, lofting up with her furious struggles. His clothing and weapons were not in sight. Wilhelm took up a fist-sized rock and staggered to his feet.

He couldn't run, but the spider moved so slowly that he was catching up even with his slow pace. It felt like he had just woken in the middle of the night and his body was still asleep. Adeline's struggles stopped as her head bounced off of a root the size of Wilhelm's thigh. Her body twisted, turning face-up as the spider climbed toward the tree.

Wilhelm's manhood twitched. Despite the desperate situation he found himself in, or maybe because of it, Adeline's supple body was affecting him. She slid over the grass and roots, her breasts rising and falling, her thighs parted by the spider's grip.

The spider.

Wilhelm growled and pushed himself forward. His arm rose above his head, and he brought the rock down with a snap and a groan. The groan was his, but the snap was the spider's leg. As the limb crumpled underneath the creature, its partner punched out at Wilhelm's unprotected side. He hadn't seen the other spider approach, and the blow on his freshly awoken body took his breath away.

Wilhelm fell onto his backside and threw his hand out to clutch Adeline's.

She was still unconscious, and her fingers slipped through his as the spider's pull took her closer to the tree. The other spider loomed, and Wilhelm kicked out, catching its diamond skin with his heel. It recoiled and hissed, then snapped forward at him. He was able to scramble away, dodging flailing downward strikes. His rock crunched into one of the thing's hands, and it shrieked. The spider backed away, clutching the injured limb to its chest.

Wilhelm risked a glance over his shoulder and saw the tree opening to accept Adeline's limp body. The spider heaved her forward, and she seemed to regain her senses just in time to scream before the tree's blackness swallowed her.

His maddened charge toward the tree made the other spider lurch away, its damaged leg hanging lifeless. Wilhelm ignored the creature as he ran. When he was still twenty feet away from the tree, he got the distinct impression that it was as big around as one of Ballenstedt's turrets. All around the tree, white bones littered the ground. One hundred men could join hands and still be unable to encircle the monstrosity.

Wilhelm didn't have a real plan, and acted on instinct, hurling his rock as a missile to keep the spider back. He jumped into the mouth of the tree and thrust his right arm forward, feeling for anything human. When his fingers found a limb of some sort, he squeezed as hard as he could, then pistoned his other arm upward. The tree's closing maw was stopped momentarily by his left arm. He pulled and was rewarded by a gurgling cry as Adeline burst forth from the viscous muck. She floundered toward him, trying to find purchase in the gore.

When he had finally pulled her close enough, Adeline threw her arms around his neck. She stared up into his eyes as Wilhelm strained against the vice of the tree's jaws.

"Thank you," she breathed.

Her kiss was like fire on his lips, and he hardly noticed when she punched his trembling arm.

The world disappeared with a crack.

§

ADELINE CLUTCHED THE MAN close, sensing his fear as they were plunged into darkness.

He's everything we had hoped for.

She kept her lips on his, which seemed to calm him somewhat. They had observed humans doing this in moments of passion, and Adeline had always thought the odd grappling of mouths an abnormal thing. Now that she experienced it in this soft human body, she understood the allure.

The Bloodtree's magic surged and bolstered her, weakening the man's resistance. Her fingers moved down his stomach. Adeline had thought she might need to use sorcery, but the man's mouth responded quickly to her own, and his hardness to her hand. While her natural form was not sexual, Adeline was a child of nature. As such, she understood the primal act of mating, but had always known it as an observer. Now, as Wilhelm's muscular body gripped her close, Adeline felt the rush of passion welling up inside herself.

She moaned as the man split her open and filled her with violent tenderness.

Adeline lost herself in their motion, in the enchantment of the Bloodtree, in the rushing blood of her human body. They existed in a tiny cocoon of pleasure, just their two souls joined by flesh.

§

WILHELM KNEW WHAT HE was doing, but he could not stop himself.

My God, forgive me my sins!

The woman's hot flesh slid against his own in a pool of blood. An abattoir of sin.

Elise, I have betrayed our vows.

His shame drove him as much as his passion. Wilhelm growled and thrust, breathing deeply of the putrid air. His lips alighted on her neck, his teeth on her nipples and shoulders. Adeline shook and moaned, her own mouth leaving trails of fire upon his skin.

Wilhelm felt the urgent climax coming and didn't resist. Something animal and raw had been awakened within him, and for a moment, he threw off the chains of morality. He existed as a man, a being of hard flesh and willpower, strong, violent, and alive.

Then, as the last of his spasms subsided, everything came crashing back.

§

ADELINE FELT THE MAN tense but didn't care. Her own pleasure had peaked into a thunderclap of sensation. He battered her while she floated on the wave of physical abandon. Then, just as suddenly as it had begun, he shoved her away. He hurled curses at her, damning her a demon, a witch, and a harlot.

The Bloodtree caught her up and carried her forward.

§

WILHELM STAGGERED FROM THE colossal tree's embrace. He fell onto the debris, snapping a bone with his knee. His body felt sated and healed — how he felt after a week of relaxation in the country with Elise. Wilhelm shuddered at the thought. He was unclean, corrupted. He had spilled his seed inside of a monster.

Would God care that it wasn't his choice?

He had to find a way out of this demonic forest, find a priest.

Behind him, the tree belched out a humanoid form. Wilhelm spun, scrambling backward like a crab. He scraped his backside multiple times; Wilhelm hoped from twigs, and not the bones. Before him, the wanton, slender shape of the witch who called herself Adeline stood, dripping dark gore. She just stared at him, her bright green eyes fixed on his flaccid manhood.

"Lord of Anhalt." The words crackled from the witch's mouth. The spiders skittered down the tree, making Wilhelm shudder again with disgust. They rose on four limbs, their uninjured arms twitching in the air.

The human-shaped demon stepped forward. The monsters clattered behind her.

"I'll be back, witches!" Wilhelm shouted, lurching to his feet. "Whatever unholy sorcery you performed on me, I will turn against you like flame to cleanse your evil from the world! I'll be back with axes and fire, soldiers and — "

"Quiet," the naked witch hissed. "You'll do nothing of the sort."

Wilhelm opened his mouth to retort, but found that he couldn't move his tongue. He balled his fists at his side. The spiders began waving their limbs and rattling in their foul tongue. Wilhelm rushed forward, intending to interrupt them, but was punched back by some unseen force.

"You'll return home to Ballenstedt. You'll forget all about what happened here. Whenever you think of the *Witchwood,* you'll feel a fear that grips your very soul. You'll encourage the people of Anhalt to leave our home alone," Adeline intoned. "Anhalt needs a strong ruler. A ruler who knows his place in the world."

Wilhelm heard the words and sneered. He turned away from the witch and her minions, toward the east. The sun was rising in the smoke-filled sky. The bishop at Ballenstedt would bless him, remove whatever spells had been placed on him.

Then he would be back.

He smiled at the promise of revenge.

Wilhelm looked back once more. The monsters were touching the human witch with their sharp limbs. The fat insects flitted around them, and Wilhelm saw the bear-things through the trees. Behind them, the huge tree swayed in the breeze.

He locked the image in his mind.

§

ADELINE STEPPED FROM THE Bloodtree, shivering in pleasure at its touch on her changed body. She saw the human on his knees among the brush and bones. Adeline had never been in a human body for as long as she would need to be for the next few seasons.

It might not be as bad as I thought.

Wilhelm turned, saw her, then scrambled backward. Adeline frowned down at him, wondering what he was about. He seemed to have an unnatural fear of her, her sisters, and their companions. They hadn't asked the humans to come into the Moonwood.

They had burned her home, cursed her with evil words.

"Lord of Anhalt." The words were still hard to force from her lips. Almut and Adelmoed scurried down the Bloodtree, joining her to bolster her courage. Adeline felt their quiet strength at her back. She sensed that they had been injured, and her anger flared.

She stepped toward the man.

"I'll be back, witches!" Wilhelm shouted, lurching to his feet.

"Whatever unholy sorcery you performed on me, I will turn against you like flame to cleanse your evil from the world! I'll be back with axes and fire, soldiers and — "

"Quiet," Adeline interrupted his foul promises. "You'll do nothing of the sort."

Adelmoed infused Adeline's words with a cantrip. The human balled his fists at his side when he realized he couldn't speak. Her sisters followed her lead, beginning the ritual that would bind their will upon the man. He rushed forward, but the Bloodtree slapped him away, then added its ancient power to their casting.

"You'll return home to Ballenstedt. You'll forget all about what happened here. Whenever you think of the *Witchwood,* you'll feel a fear that grips your very soul. You'll encourage the people of Anhalt to leave our home alone," Adeline chanted, inserting the words, and their meaning, into the human's subconscious. "Anhalt needs a strong ruler. A ruler who knows his place in the world."

As she finished, she moved her hands to her stomach. To the new life growing there.

The man stumbled away, moving east.

He turned back once more, smiling. Adeline met his smile with one of her own, her hand upon her belly, her sisters rubbing her soft back and shoulders. Her fairies, the few still alive, flitted around them, cheering their victory. Adelmoed's creatures sulked in the trees, not joining the celebration.

§

WILHELM EXITED THE WOOD as the morning sun forced the shadows from the sky. He began walking west, toward Ballenstedt.

Toward home.

AUTHOR KOLIN GATES

KOLIN GATES writes hard-edged fantasy with heroic moral undertones; horror that follows you to bed at night; and emotional, thought-provoking science fiction. He writes the kind of books and stories that he wants to read, and puts his heart into each one.

You can find more info about all of his writing in one place: www.kolingates.com.

FAE TOUCHED

HEATHER MARIE ADKINS

CHAPTER ONE

*F**uck, it's hot.*

My sweaty palm slipped on my gun. I eased down the creaky hall, flinching at every squeak of the boards beneath my feet. Even after nearly a decade in law enforcement, my heart still beat wildly, a frightened bird seeking exit from my rib cage.

I stopped before the hallway tee'd and glanced across at my partner as he slid into place. His stance mirrored mine — feet wide, back to the wall, senses on alert, gun down, safety off.

Dirk Carrington was ten years my junior and a helluva lot prettier than me with his shiny, coiffed black hair and dimples, but he made a damn fine cop. It could have been my own bias, of course. I'd been his field training officer two years ago, and it showed. I'd molded him into what I expected from a cop, and we made a great team, which is why I was no longer his FTO, but his partner.

Dirk took one hand off his gun to *vee* two fingers at his eyes before pointing around the corner.

I nodded and lifted my gun, taking an imperceptible breath before I leapt into the next hallway.

Empty.

Fuck. The guy *had to be* here. Carrington and I had watched him enter through the broken side door less than five minutes before. We'd secured the first floor — no basement — and then moved upstairs. If he wasn't on this floor, he'd done a disappearing act even Harry Houdini would have appreciated.

We'd been monitoring this abandoned house for months trying to catch this creep. The guy was smoke and mirrors, disappearing at whim and reappearing long enough to be seen kidnapping yet another toddler — none of whom had been found, dead or alive. I was beyond ready to take this sicko down. Taking the teary, red-eyed statements of young parents who'd lost hope their child was even alive had started to wear on me.

I kept my gun on a closed door at the far end of the hallway and motioned for Carrington to head the other way. A well-oiled machine, we were, checking rooms silently, listening for any indication we weren't alone in the house. I remained hyper-aware of Carrington's location as we searched, ready to run to his aid if the need arose.

This house hadn't been occupied since Nixon held office. Each room yielded only four walls and bad 70s shag carpet. Our intel told us the family who owned the place lived in Los Angeles, which meant the old downtown brownstone was as forgotten as a Lost Boy.

I finally made it to the closed door at the end of the hallway. Something told me this was it; I'd find our perp. It could have been instinct — I'd long ago learned to trust my gut, because it rarely steered me wrong. But it could also have been because the guy had *literally* nowhere else to hide.

I paused for a split second to consider waiting for Carrington. I glanced back through the gloom but met only silence and stillness. The clock ticked forward like a death knell.

I trained my gun on the door and turned the knob.

The perp stood dead-center of yet another empty bedroom, his arms lifted towards the ceiling. A vicious wind whipped around him, turning wild his curtain of blond hair. He spoke, chanting something in a language I didn't recognize.

The most recent kidnapped child sat at his feet, reaching for the wind with an innocent smile.

I entered the room and braced myself against the out-of-place, inside hurricane, trying not to think too hard about *why* it was happening. "Freeze!"

In the same moment I heard Carrington's heavy boots begin to race down the hallway, the perp turned and pointed at me with a pale, luminescent hand.

Something hot hit me in the chest and knocked me from my feet. I got off a shot — wide, but it hit the guy in the shoulder, and that was better than nothing.

I hit the floor of the bedroom hard, my breath *whoosh*ing out of me. My gun skittered across the hardwood and came to rest against the far wall. Whatever had hit me, hit my Kevlar vest instead, and did little damage.

"Cromwell!" My partner's voice was closer out in the hallway. Someone who didn't know him like I did would never have heard the panic in his tone.

I shook away the cobwebs, rolling to face the open door. Carrington appeared, but the wind slammed the door in his face, locking him outside.

The monsoon calmed dramatically as the perp touched his shoulder, his hand coming away stained with purple.

Purple? What the hell?

"You will pay for that," he said calmly, an exotic accent to his melodic voice.

I got my first look at his eyes, as green as the first growth of grass in spring. They glinted cold, nearly inhuman.

The door shuddered as my partner slammed his shoulder into the wood.

"He's gonna get in," I said smugly. Remain confident, and thus keep the pursued on guard. Also, it helps to not look like a loser when prone on the floor.

The perp snarled then turned his back on me, lifting his arms and starting in on the gibberish again. The wind howled to life as if commanded, and the air crackled with energy: the electricity of a storm brewing.

I launched across the room for my gun, but a brilliant flash of light knocked me off course. I hit the wall head first, and stars burst in my vision. For what seemed an eternity, I couldn't see through the blinding pain. Black edged my periphery. I clung to consciousness like a drowning woman.

When I could finally see again, I was absolutely certain I had a concussion. That certainty was solidified upon what I saw thereafter.

Swirling colors on the opposite wall opened like a portal in a science fiction movie. The kidnapper scooped the child into his arms and moved forward without sparing me another glance.

I didn't have time to think or strategize. I *knew* if I let him walk through that swirling vortex, the toddler would be lost. I could try to save the kid — and possibly injure him in the process — or I could let them go and another mother would mourn.

I shoved off the wall, lurched to my feet, and barreled into the guy.

I twisted all five-foot-three, one-hundred-twenty pounds of me, dragging the much taller, thicker man around to land on top of me. The move hurt me like all hell, but the toddler safely landed on the perp and slid from his arms to the floor.

The door splintered but didn't break as Carrington continued to slam into it. God damn old houses, made to withstand the god damn apocalypse.

"I could use a little help!" I yelled, struggling to roll the perp off me with my stronger leg muscles.

"I'm trying!" Carrington snapped, hitting the door so hard bits of plaster rained from the ceiling.

The perp twisted on top of me, reaching for my throat. The weird purple liquid oozing from his gunshot wound dripped onto my face, burning like acid. My body flared hot, radiating from the point where the liquid melted onto my skin.

I wrestled the man with everything I had, but his hands clamped like vises around my neck. I fought to breathe, to remain conscious and battling.

If I gave up, I was dead.

The door finally splintered from the frame and flew open. Carrington hurled into the room, gun aloft and a slew of curse words rolling off his tongue.

The perp rolled me so that I was on top of him — smart move, because my partner couldn't take a shot without endangering me. I hated intelligent criminals. They were few and far between, but man, they really made my job difficult.

I sucked in precious air at the absence of his death grip.

With a mighty shove, the perp tossed me across the room like a missile. I hit Carrington, and we crumpled to a pile of arms and legs. Dirk shoved me off him — quite painfully, I might add — and aimed for the kidnapper, getting off a shot before the guy jumped through the vortex and disappeared.

The swirling colors vanished.

The wind died.

And I lost consciousness.

CHAPTER TWO

I'd woken up in a hospital once before, when I'd taken a metal chair to the noggin during a bar room brawl. That was the first — and last — time I worked security for a bar.

When I opened my eyes this time, Carrington grinned. "Hey, tiger. How's the head?"

He sat in a chair next to my hospital bed, his feet propped up on the blankets beside me and the remote in his hand. He was casual in a pair of khaki cargo shorts and a T-shirt that declared him *Off-duty cop working on a case* atop a sketch of a 24-pack.

"Your wife know you're playing hooky?" I asked, easing up on the bed. Maybe it was my deep desire to always be in control, but I didn't like my younger partner seeing me laid up like an invalid.

Carrington hit a button on the bedside remote and the bed slowly rose. I waved a hand when my body reached a good angle. He handed me the remote and clasped his hands behind his head. "The wife's at her mother's with Darla. Yard sale-ing."

"It's Friday. Who does yard sales on Fridays?"

"Actually, it's Saturday."

I stared at him, noticing the dark circles under his eyes. "I've been out more than a day?"

"Give or take a few hours. How's your head?" he asked again.

I paused to take stock of my injuries. "Aches," I said honestly. I winked one eye shut, then the other. Carrington's face remained blurry either way. "I can't see really well."

"Doc said to expect that. You had a nasty concussion. How the hell did you manage to tackle a full grown man with a concussion?"

"Sheer force of willpower." I grinned, and the movement made my chin and cheek burn. I cupped my jaw with a hand. "Ow. What's wrong with my face?"

Carrington took a deep breath and reached for his phone. He pulled up his camera and put it on the face setting, then handed it over. "They aren't really sure. The perp dripped something on you. Acid or something. They took a skin scrape to test."

I stared at my image on the screen. A jagged purple line stretched from my cheekbone to my ear, and all the way down my neck. The skin around it shone angry and red.

"Hurts like hell. Worse than my head, I think." I handed his phone back.

"Any idea what it was?"

I thought back to the guy's hot blood burning my face. But that was crazy. Right? His blood didn't *literally* burn me. Instead of answering, I stalled. "Who sent the flowers?"

Carrington glanced over his shoulder at the two dozen red and white roses sitting lonely on the windowsill. A white card jutted from the bushel. He cleared his throat. "One guess."

"I swear to god, if they're from Jacob, I'll shoot him with my department-issued weapon and a smile on my face."

Carrington grimaced. "In that case, I will neither confirm nor deny that they are from your ex-husband."

"He never gives up."

"Come on, Lara. He had a good woman, and he fucked up. He's trying to make it right."

"He should have made it right before I filed for divorce." I rubbed my cheek. "Fuck. Hurts to even talk."

"Did he hit you with something? Acid?"

I stared at my partner, weighing how much to say. He knew I was evading the question. He'd be like a damn dog on a scent until I answered him. "What did you see when you came in the room?"

He stayed silent so long I wondered if he was going to answer me. He met my gaze. "I'm... not sure."

"What do you mean you're *not sure*?"

"What I saw can't be explained."

"Explain it anyway."

"There was a hole in the wall made of... colors. He jumped through it. The hole disappeared." Even as he spoke, it was obvious he didn't quite believe his eyes.

I touched the raw skin on my face. "It's his blood. I think. I mean, it came from where I shot him. But it wasn't red."

"So... what? The guy wasn't human or something? That's impossible. It was a trick of light or stage magic — "

"Dirk, be real," I cut him off. "If you can't trust your own eyes, what can you trust? We saw the same thing. He opened that vortex in the wall by waving his hands and muttering some incantation. I watched it happen."

"You hit your head," Carrington argued.

"I'm going to hit *your* head," I griped. "Don't be an idiot. You know what we saw was real."

"I don't know, Lara. It was *un*real."

"Real enough," I said, tracing the tender line of purple on my jaw.

§

"THIS IS EXACTLY WHY I wish you'd been a teacher," my mother remarked as she turned over the engine on her Mercedes and pulled out of the parking garage.

"Ma, come on," I said wearily. Early Saturday afternoon sunshine filled the car as we accelerated up the interstate ramp. The gauge on my mother's car read 98°, and it would probably reach one hundred before dinner. I slumped against the passenger window, dressed in the gray sweats and hoodie she'd brought me from my apartment. I felt like shit but had a prescription in my pocket for something to help me sleep.

"Lara, you are a woman, but you sure don't act like one."

"Jesus H., Ma. Tons of women are cops." I closed my eyes. Maybe if I pretended to sleep, we wouldn't have to have this conversation again.

My mother took pride in being a true Southern belle. She kept her blonde curls sprayed and primped in an elegant chignon, and her makeup was always perfect no matter the day or time. She was a lady, and as such, expected *me* to be a lady.

Needless to say, my choice of career irritated her as much as the fact that I preferred beer over wine and pizza over country club caviar.

Mom patted my leg with a hand manicured in red claws. "At least come home and let me take care of you. I'll make you meatloaf for dinner."

"I just want to go back to my place and sleep with my cat."

My mother sighed — the same sigh she used every time I failed to live up to her expectations. "I blame your father. You shouldn't be thirty-three years old, living alone in an apartment with only a cat."

"You blame Dad for everything. Maybe I should have called him to pick me up instead."

"You hush your mouth. There's a beautiful bouquet of roses in the backseat from a man who is desperate to win you back. And you told me to trash them."

"I told you to chop them into little pieces and scatter them on his front steps. Big difference in tactics." I grinned but didn't open my eyes. I could feel her glare, anyway.

"I love you, darling, but you're gonna be the death of me."

"The feeling is mutual," I murmured, willing myself to drift to sleep.

CHAPTER THREE

*T*he dead of night found me on the couch, Sassy-the-cat on my chest, and my painkillers wearing off. I awoke from dreams of swirling color and dripping purple blood. My face still burned, the skin around the strange mark angry and tight. The purple seemed to have faded a little the last time I went to the bathroom, but the pain had not.

I ran a hand over Sassy's black fur, taking comfort in her purrs. Darkness pressed in on us like a blanket. I slid back into sleep, still conscious of her rumbles on my torso, but my body bleeding purple in my dreams.

I startled awake as light flooded the room.

A drop-dead gorgeous man with amethyst eyes and dark chocolate hair in a smooth ponytail stood by the light switch. He bowed, his eyes never leaving mine. He was clothed in black, a holster hanging around his long, lean torso, gun securely locked in place.

I leapt to my feet, reaching for my own firearm on the coffee table.

The man waved a hand, and my gun flew across the room — *by itself.* He waved again, and an unseen force pressed me back into the cushions, my legs splayed and my fluffy kitten-patterned socks on display.

"Cease and desist, woman. I'm not here to hurt you." He held a palm toward me, his face grim. "Are you Officer Lara Cromwell of the Savannah police?"

"Let me go!" I snapped, certain he held me down even though his hand was nowhere near me. What the hell was happening with me? First, swirling vortexes, now, a man using telekinesis to hold me down. Clearly, someone needed to lock me away in a looney bin. Someone tell my mother her wish would come true. I probably wouldn't be a cop after all this was said and done, because they'd deem me insane.

"Please answer the question. The ritual must be fulfilled if you wish to live."

I raised an eyebrow. "You're not here to hurt me, huh?"

He sighed and rolled his eyes. "Are you Officer Lara Cromwell of the Savannah police?"

"Yeah, yeah."

"A full sentence, please."

"Oh, for fuck's sake." I struggled against his hold and collapsed into the cushions when he didn't move a muscle. "Fine. I am Officer Lara Cromwell of the Savannah police."

"Did you or did you not shoot a man two days ago?"

"I did."

"And he bled on you?"

"So it *was* blood?" I asked, staring at the intruder expectantly. "The purple stuff?"

"Answer the question, Miss Cromwell."

"Yes, the man bled purple shit on me."

A muscle moved in the intruder's jaw. If I didn't know any better, I'd think he was holding back a laugh. "Officer Cromwell, you are now a sidhe. We have much to discuss, and my department requires your assistance. Will you come with me?"

"*She?*" I asked.

"Sidhe. Humans refer to us by many names: fae, fairy, elves, brownies. Whatever you wish to call us, you are now one of us. But you must come with me and have the food of our table if you wish to survive the transformation."

"Whoa, whoa." I sat up, and the pressure on my chest faded as he lowered his hand. "These painkillers are crazy. You are a figment of my imagination, and I respectfully request that you vacate my head. Now. Please." I wobbled a little as I stood, my head wavery and heavy on my neck, and stumbled for the kitchen.

I needed water. Lots of it splashed on my face, maybe with a little ice in it to really give me that kick.

My figment followed, his steps swift and silent. That's when I knew he really *was* imaginary. No man could look that good, smell that wonderful, and function like a damn ninja.

As I turned on the faucet in the kitchen, I glanced at his feet and realized he trailed silvery dust across my floors as he walked. I let the cool water fill my hands and said, "You're getting my floors dirty."

He gave me a look like I'd insulted his mother. "Fairy dust is not 'dirty.' It will fade in time."

"My floors aren't going to fly away to Neverland, are they?"

He chuckled. "No, but as a matter of fact, Mr. J.M. Barrie was himself a fairy."

"Barrie the fairy." I snorted, splashing copious amounts of cool water on my face. My purple mark burned something wicked.

"Ms. Cromwell, I don't think you're taking this as seriously as you should." He crossed the kitchen so fast I didn't see him move. He gripped my arms — gently, thank God, or I would have been forced to lay him out on the tiles and make him bleed — and turned me to face him. "You *must* come with me now. Your fate depends on it."

I yanked from his grasp and took a step back, water dripping from my face. He smelled *too* good, like cinnamon and honey and maybe something stronger, like single-malt whiskey. The scent was doing things to my body it shouldn't have. "So you're telling me because the kidnapper bled on me, I'm going to turn into a fairy."

"That is correct."

"Am I going to sprout wings? Trail pixie dust from the bottom of my Nikes?" I motioned to his feet, only just realizing his silver dust came from military issue combat boots. What a bizarre combination.

"You will not sprout wings. Only the fae born with wings have them."

"So not all fairies fly?"

"No."

"What about the pixie dust?"

He sighed, his strong jaw clenching twice before he answered. "It is not pixie dust. It is fairy dust. Pixies are born, not made. Yes, you will begin to shed the dust, but only if you complete the transformation."

"What does the dust do?"

"Consider it a 'fingerprint,' of sorts. Of your magic."

I took another step back, catching my hip on the kitchen counter. "I'm going to do magic?"

"Only if you come with me and complete the transformation." He held out a hand, palm up. His skin was scuffed and worn; his hands had seen several go-rounds with the years. I liked that in a man.

"I don't have to complete the transformation?" I asked, relief flooding me. "'Cause no thanks. I like my life. I don't want to leak pixie dust in my police cruiser."

"Ms. Cromwell. Please listen to me, as we haven't much time."

I shut my mouth. "Fine. I'm listening."

"You can choose to not complete the transformation. However, that will result in your death, and my department will lose the only lead we've had on Arrowroot Callahan in months."

I processed "result in your death," but arrived at "What the hell's an Arrowroot Callahan?"

That damn muscle in his jaw ticked again, and his amethyst eyes sparkled. "You are an odd woman."

"I'm a cop. What did you expect, a Disney princess?"

"You have exceeded all my expectations." He chuckled, but sobered quickly, catching my gaze. "Will you come with me?"

"What's Arrowroot Callahan?"

"Who. He is the fae who bled on you."

"The one stealing toddlers," I clarified.

"The very same."

I eyed him, looking for any indication he was lying to me. I was usually pretty good at knowing when people were trying to fleece me; it's a skill developed by years of slinging handcuffs on criminals. But my system held enough painkillers to stun a small thoroughbred, and my head pounded like drums at a rock concert. Sure, there was the off-chance I was dreaming. Hallucinating, maybe.

But I'd seen enough weird shit in the last forty-eight hours to make me shrug and say, "Let me get my gun."

"Guns are not allowed on sidhe land except by sidhe enforcement officers."

I crossed my arms, well-aware my intimidation levels were adversely affected by my kitten socks and the holes in my Spongebob Squarepants sweatshirt. "I am a law enforcement officer and, to hear you tell it, I'll be sidhe once I go with you and 'have the food of your table.'"

"You do listen."

I ignored his dig and his stupid, sexy smile. "So therefore, I'm a soon-to-be sidhe enforcement officer by default. I take my gun or no deal."

His jaw twitched. "At least change into something less... pineapple-under-the-sea."

I burst out laughing. "I'm impressed. You know your cartoons."

"I'm fae, not dead. We like your TV, too."

"I don't even know your name."

He straightened his shoulders and offered me a hand. "Major Drago Stormfire of the Sidhe Enforcement Unit. Special Investigations."

I accepted his handshake, his warm palm enveloping mine. Something fiery passed between us, and I couldn't stop my squeak of surprise.

Drago Stormfire either didn't feel it or had top-notch suppression skills. "I'll wait for you in the living room. Welcome aboard, Officer Cromwell."

CHAPTER FOUR

 *J*une in Georgia meant sweating the moment I stepped outside. I tugged at my tank top, trying to get some air flowing before my boobs drowned. "Can't you just open a vortex like that Callahan dude and get us to sidhe on my dining room wall?"

Drago coughed, but I'm pretty sure there was a laugh in there. "I could, but your body isn't equipped to travel temporary portals. Yet."

I shuddered. "Don't say 'yet' like that."

"Like what?"

"Like it's a threat."

He glanced at me, his face in shadow as we left the orange glow of the streetlamp and walked toward the park across the street. The heat left from the day emanated from the asphalt, burning the soles of my sneakers. Thank god I'd chosen cut off shorts, or Drago Stormfire would be mopping me off Rowan Street.

"Becoming fae is not a threat," he snapped. "It is a privilege. One you are obviously not prepared to take on."

"Whoa, buddy." I jerked to a stop and held up both hands. "Rein that temper in. I was perfectly fine carrying a badge, a gun, and the human genome until your boy Arrowroot decided to share his blood with me and change my life."

"I doubt the choice was his," Drago intoned dramatically. "If it were I, I'd have chosen a much better candidate."

"Watch it, bud. I'm carrying." I patted my holster, dangling in plain sight over my tank top.

Drago patted his own gun, and the sight did things to my nether regions. "As am I."

I couldn't help but wonder what *else* he was *carrying*. Jesus, was I getting turned on by a hot guy packing heat?

The fairy man led me towards the geometrical dome on the playground. I remembered playing on it as a kid — maybe not this one, exactly, but ones like it. The dome arose from the ground in pentagonal patterns, reaching a height of nearly eight feet. A little high, it seemed to me, but I wasn't a parent, so what did I know?

Drago waved a hand and a section of the dome wavered from existence, leaving a Drago-sized hole. He passed through, but I remained rooted to the well-worn dirt.

"Is there a problem?" Drago asked, his tone making it clear whatever *problem* I had would fall short of his desire to fix it.

"Can you just wave a hand and do anything you want?"

"Mostly. I couldn't wave a hand and make you disappear, so clearly I can't do *anything* I want." He smirked.

"You've got spunk, I'll give you that," I muttered, stomping through the hole.

"Likewise, Ms. Cromwell."

As I passed where the bars had been, the faintest brush of energy crackled along my body, like a phantom memory. Once I joined him, Drago waved an enigmatic hand and closed the hole.

"We could have just crawled through the holes like a normal kid," I said.

"I do not crawl," Drago responded airily. He began to stomp in the bare dirt beneath the center of the dome.

I watched him, amused. "You play in the dirt. Can't be much different."

He shot me an irritated glare, feet still moving. "This is in intricate dance wherein tempo and cadence opens the portal to sidhe."

"You're stomping. In the dirt."

"Please stop talking. I cannot concentrate."

I managed three seconds of silence before I had to remark, "I think your rain dance is defective, Tonto. I don't see any storm clouds."

Drago stomped so hard dust kicked up around his ankles. He looked up, his body eerily still after all that shaking and jiving. Beneath his feet, the ground began a rainbow swirl. "You are an infuriating woman."

"Likewise, Mr. Stormfire." I smiled prettily.

A strong, sinewy arm shot through the space between us, fingers bruising as he jerked me to him. I stumbled over my feet and fell against his chest, his other hand moving to my bicep to steady me.

I leaned against Drago's muscles, skin growing as hot as when Arrowroot Callahan's purple blood dripped on my face but for entirely different reasons. Abs so chiseled I could cut myself pressed against my body, and a delicious view of his gorgeous face loomed over me.

"Hold your breath," Drago murmured, his voice vibrating through my torso and awakening things in me that hadn't seen the light of day since college.

No worries, I thought. I had already forgotten how to breathe cradled like a woman in his bedroom.

We sank so fast it took my stomach. Suddenly, the colors that had been growing beneath us were all around us, dizzying and intense. Only Drago's steady hands kept me grounded as we fell into the abyss.

It ended quickly, our boots touching down on stone floors as the colors faded into memory. In the sudden stillness, I realized my chest was so tight against Drago's torso that my breasts spilled quite a bit of cleavage over my top. His amethyst gaze alerted me to the escape.

I let go of the man as if he were fire itself, and busied myself adjusting my tank top and checking for my gun. All lethal weapons accounted for, inside and outside my shirt.

Drago cleared his throat. "Ah, yes. The first portal travel is indeed disorienting. You'll get used to it. Follow me."

"Where are we?" I asked, keeping my steps light as I rushed to keep up. Stone surrounded us on all sides, but the floors shone as if recently polished. Torches flickered from the walls, casting shadows over Drago's face. It was blessedly cool after the stifling oven of Savannah at night.

"The basement of the Sidhe Enforcement Agency in Sector 22. My department."

We turned a dim corner, and the hall opened into a foyer. A dark office sat enclosed by glass doors, desks empty and silent. Drago moved away from the office toward a wide staircase, and we ascended.

"A branch of the faery police opens up beneath a children's playground?" I clarified with a snort.

"Not specifically." Drago shot me an irritated look. "The portals are like elevators we control with our minds. I open it from its physical placement in your reality, but it takes us wherever I demand."

"That would be convenient for cops back home."

"It is a fae magick not meant for human use. When you are given the privilege of learning it, you would do well to remember that."

"Super-secret passages. Got it."

The stairs spilled us into an atrium that bustled with a lot more life than the basement. Uniformed officers strolled in and out the massive front doors, beyond which a storm raged in a busy street. The gray light indicated day, which was odd considering we had left the darkest hours of night behind us to get here. I pointed outside.

"Time does not exist in faery," Drago answered my unspoken question.

"How can time not exist? Isn't it just…a thing?"

"You cannot misconstrue human constructs as valid in this realm. The human world is not true reality. It is an existence created, mapped, and utterly categorized by man. It is a falsification."

We stopped outside a metal door labeled *Consultation 3* in shiny silver letters. The torchlight here was less prominent than in the basement; opaque globes surrounded the open flames, but they still reflected in Drago's amethyst eyes.

"You're telling me the life and world I know aren't real. Are you trying to get me on your side or are you trying to push me away? Because right now, I'm not a fan of you."

Drago lifted a sardonic brow. It arched with a perfection not even the best stylist could have waxed. "Miss Cromwell, I will not sugarcoat the truth. This is your reality now, and it is the correct one. Consider it this way," — He grasped the doorknob. — "before your exposure to Callahan blood, you slept. Now, your eyes are open."

He opened the door and disappeared inside. I had no choice but to follow.

§

CONSULTATION 3, RATHER THAN being a sterile interrogation room with a two-way mirror and chairs chained to the floor, looked more like a medieval dining hall. Opaque globes on the walls illuminated a long wooden table set with food. Giant gold mirrors reflected light and people — men and women in Sidhe Enforcement blues. If it weren't for the presence of glittering wings and pastel skin colors, we could have been interrupting any LEO board meeting back home.

A gray-haired woman at the head of the table stood, her high-backed chair screeching over stone. She looked at me, perplexed. "This is her?"

The distaste in her tone was not amusing.

"This is me," I retorted before Drago could speak.

He sent me a glare before he smiled easily at the woman. "This is her. Don't let her appearance fool you, Narcissa. She may be petite and of great beauty, but she has the heart and attitude of a lioness."

I barely heard anything he said after "great beauty." My cheeks burned with embarrassment, a little because of Drago's compliment and a little because of the shrewd gazes eyeing me with interest. As if I *were* a lioness. In a cage. Obviously, these people didn't realize how dangerous a caged lion could be.

I bared my teeth at the gaping crowd as Drago pulled out a chair and offered it to me. "Please, have a seat, Miss Cromwell."

"I'll stand."

Drago lifted one perfect brow. "Miss Cromwell."

It wasn't a question or a demand, but it was clear he meant for me to obey. His twinkling lavender eyes said *Be a good girl*.

I didn't find myself inclined to be a good girl, simply because the gray-haired fairy still eyeballed me with derision. But I *was* intrigued, and I wanted answers. Not just to the question of my sudden faery lineage, but also to why Arrowroot Callahan was helping himself to human toddlers.

I winked at Drago and smoothly took the chair. I affected a fainting rose southern accent. "Why, thank you, kind sir."

A snort drifted from the opposite side of the table from a stocky guy with buzzed blond hair and eyes that swirled a rainbow of colors. He offered me a friendly thumbs-up and then turned his attention back to old gray-head.

She cleared her throat, still standing as she rested the tips of her fingers on the edge of the table. She didn't appear the least bit otherworldly in her bulky uniform and no-nonsense ponytail. "Welcome, Miss Cromwell. Drago has hopefully updated you to your current predicament — "

"Have the food of your table or die," I cut in.

"Ah- um. Yes." She pressed her surprisingly plump lips together in a thin, irritated line. Obviously, the Queen Bee didn't appreciate her spotlight stolen. "As you can see, we have an array of dishes here for you to choose from. I am sorry to say, my unit has already dined, and I apologize if the food has grown cold." She glanced at Drago. "We expected you two hours ago."

"I encountered difficulties."

Such a politically correct answer, seeing as his "difficulties" were me.

I spoke again, electing to use the syrupy-sweet drawl my mama used to deal with women she disliked. "I'm sorry. You seem to know *my* name, but have yet to give me yours."

The lady looked stumped, as if she weren't used to people not knowing her identity. Such things as introductions were anathema in her world, apparently. "Commander Narcissa Wingroot. I am the unit commander for Sector 22 of the Sidhe Enforcement Agency."

I glanced at Drago in surprise. He wore leadership like a fucking mantel on his shoulders, the way Superman wore his cape. But it appeared he wasn't in charge. My initial impression had been wrong. That concussion really *had* rattled my brains.

Narcissa inclined her head. "Miss Cromwell, I welcome you to help yourself. Eat while we debrief you on the current investigation into Arrowroot Callahan. You will have no need to speak."

She may as well have told me to shut up and eat.

So I did.

CHAPTER FIVE

I thought my first buttery bite of croissant would be followed by a huge shift in consciousness. Some kind of dramatization to indicate I was no longer completely human, that my life would forever change beneath a veil of fairy dust. A ringing bell, a heavenly light, a chorus to sing my ode... *Something.*

Instead, I delighted in how tasty the roll was — hints of cinnamon? Nutmeg? I wasn't much of a cook. — and moved on to the mashed potatoes, crusty flakes on my fingertips and Wingroot's voice in my ears.

How anti-climactic.

"Miss Cromwell," Wingroot started, still looming over the table. "Nearly five generations ago, a debilitating illness struck our people."

Looking up at her gave me a crick in the neck. I got the message — she was the woman in charge, and being in charge meant standing above everyone else. Not my personal way of leadership, but to each their own bad habits.

Narcissa continued. "This illness swept through the females of our race. While we experienced no significant loss of life at that time, something far worse occurred."

Ah, finally, the answer to a fate worse than death, I thought, suppressing an eye roll. I shoved another bite of croissant in my mouth and remained mute. Respect the faeries, for they are people, too. Or something.

"This illness targeted the genetic line of our people," Wingroot intoned, voice impassioned, face expressionless. "Over the next decade, it came to light that the women of faery could no longer bear children."

I glanced at her, my fork resting in a pile of cinnamon apples. A touch of sadness graced her steely eyes and made me feel shitty for my uncharitable thoughts. Because yeah — extinction of an entire race *would* seem a fate worse than death.

Narcissa cleared her throat, the ambivalent shroud repositioning on her handsome face. "It has been almost a century since the plague, and our numbers are dwindling. In all of fae, an average of six babes survive to term each year. We are in danger, Miss Cromwell."

"But I was turned by blood," I said, forgetting my order to stay quiet and let the boss speak. "Can't you just find humans willing to transition?"

"The blood change requires an open mind and a belief in the fae most humans do not possess."

"I don't — *didn't* believe in fae," I said. "Yet here I am."

"Obviously, some part of you did, or you would not be here," Narcissa responded. Across from me, Drago nodded his agreement.

I didn't have a response to that. I thought a girl knew her own mind, but maybe not. Maybe our minds know *us*.

"In any case, the blood change does not make one a full sidhe, Miss Cromwell." Narcissa's nose tipped up ever-so-slightly as she gazed at me. "Your transformation is honorary. You remain human but possess the more desirable qualities of the fae. You are not the blood of our people. You are... let us say 'fae touched.'"

That sounded like a bad paranormal romance novel.

"Callahan is kidnapping human children," I pointed out. Physically, with my fork. At her hawk-like nose. "That tells me humans are worth something, at least. But only as children?"

Narcissa, to her credit, appeared surprised and a little pleased at my powers of deduction. "And so, Miss Cromwell. Human toddlers, specifically those below the age of five human years, can be completely transformed. Changelings, we call them. In those pre-dawn years, human children are not closed to the fae realm. A metaphysical door within their minds allows for a full change. They are no longer human at all after a blood bond."

I detected something in her voice — longing? Pride? A weird combination of both? I put down my fork and studied her. The rest of the group waited in what seemed to be breathless anticipation. Drago looked smug, as if he had faith in my investigative skills.

For good reason.

I caught Narcissa's strong gaze. "You were a Changeling."

She inclined her head. "Many, many years ago. Long before our race began to falter."

I resumed my eating and spoke through a mouth full of potatoes. "Seems to me Callahan is doing what he thinks is necessary to preserve the population. So why is he wanted?"

"We may be in trouble, Miss Cromwell, but that does not mean we are monsters."

Oh, there was that haughtiness. I thought she'd lost it.

"We have strict laws regarding Changelings. They must be orphaned. They must be in danger. Or they must be given to us willingly by the human mother who bore them."

I thought of the teary faces I'd interviewed for weeks on end, my heart bending beneath their grief as our department tried desperately to track smoke. "None of that applies to the children Callahan has taken."

"And thus why we are attempting to stop him."

"Were you orphaned?" I asked.

Narcissa pursed her lips. "I don't see how that is any of your business, Miss Cromwell."

"I'm sorry," I told her honestly. Sorry for my question, sorry for whatever she'd lost.

"Why me?" I addressed Drago this time, tired of his smug silence. "Other than saving my life by giving me 'the food of your table,'" My imitation of his clipped accent elicited a brief twitch of his luscious lips, "why am I here? You came for me. Called me a 'lead' on Callahan. Why?"

"As bluntly as you read Commander Wingroot's heritage, surely you already know the answer to that question."

I stared at him, briefly distracted by the quirk of his lips. Red. Smooth. Kissable. "I have a connection to Callahan."

"A blood bond," Narcissa cut in. "More than a connection. It's a metaphysical relationship, like that of father and child. It is permanent. In-severable."

My fork clattered to my plate, taking my appetite with it. The smug look on Drago's face — the one I thought was pride over the way I proved myself to the commander — had vanished. In its place rested an expression much too close to pity.

I didn't like pity, particularly when directed at me.

I shoved my plate away and clapped my hands. "All right, kids. What next? Do I just think of him real hard and click my heels together? Chant 'Home, sweet, Arrowroot'?"

Drago coughed — hiding a smile, no doubt. He was good at that.

Narcissa seemed to visibly brace herself, as if fighting a deep need to order me out of her department. "It isn't as simple as that, Miss Cromwell. The blood bond is a connection that takes many years to master, usually under the tutelage of the one who changed you."

"Well we don't have time for that, commander. Plus, if I'm close enough to be under Callahan's tutelage, I'm gonna shoot, not learn my multiplication tables."

Narcissa glared at Drago who held his hands up in defeat, but he winked at me when she looked away.

"The abbreviated version," I said. "Accelerated program-style."

Narcissa closed her eyes briefly and took a breath. Probably in lieu of strangling me. "As I am the only officer on this department who has experienced a blood bond, I shall be the one to train you on how to harness the power and locate Callahan."

I suppressed an urge to groan.

She looked as if she smelled something rotten. Good — she was as happy as I was at the thought of private, one-on-one girl time.

"We will begin tomorrow at eight a.m.," she finished. "Drago can show you to your quarters."

"My quarters?" I shook my head. "I'll do what I can to help, but I have a perfectly good apartment and a perfectly comfy bed with a cat and painkillers waiting for m — " I stopped.

Pain. I felt no pain. My vision was crisp as a brand new dollar bill. I fingered the spot where my head had made contact with the wall — the goose egg beneath my scalp was gone.

I stood, striding quickly to one of the gilded mirrors hanging along the wall beside a dormant fireplace. The Lara Cromwell who stared back at me looked better than she had in years. My cheeks were rosy. My skin glowing. My usually lank hair as golden as fine corn silk.

And the angry purple stain on my face from Callahan's blood had disappeared.

The thin, translucent scar above my eyebrow I'd gotten falling off a fence in my first year policing — gone.

The spider web of scars on the inside of my wrist from a dog attack on duty three years ago — vanished.

The dark brown birthmark on my collarbone — history.

If I'd wanted to give a show to my fellow law enforcement officers, I could have dropped trou' and checked the crescent-shaped scar on my ass cheek, but I would just assume it was gone, too. A good thing, considering its origins were embarrassing.

For a brief moment, lost in my wonder, I had forgotten I wasn't alone. Then Drago drew up behind me, his spicy-whiskey scent intoxicating and his amethyst eyes on me.

"Human," he said, voice low, pitched only for my ears, "but with the best of fae. The new Lara Cromwell."

I shivered; not over the implications of a new life, but over the charcoal glide of my name on his lips.

CHAPTER SIX

"*I* would sleep for a week if Commander Vader wasn't gonna stomp her boots on my doorstep at the crack of dawn." I yawned, keeping my stride long and even with Drago's as we crossed my street, aiming for my apartment building.

"You did well, though I'll admit, I did not have high hopes for you."

"Thanks," I said dryly.

"Narcissa is…" he trailed off, as if lost for the correct adjective.

"Beastly?"

He coughed.

"Ghastly? Horrendous? Egocentric? Please stop me if I reach the right word. I could keep going."

"*Hard to please,*" Drago said, not without a little amusement.

Okay, so I got a rush knowing I could make him smile. I'd been surrounded by men for the better part of a decade. And cops… well, they're crude, rude, and down with the morbid humor. Believe me, I wasn't complaining — I was no better. But Drago wasn't anything like the men I knew. Quiet. Polite.

So hot I'd melt in his presence if the Savannah summer didn't kill me first.

The cool A/C of my apartment building rushed out as we entered. Drago held the heavy glass door open for me. We climbed the stairs in silence, me *way* too aware of his presence, and Drago much too unreadable.

Outside my door, we faced each other.

"She'll be here early," Drago told me. "I know how she operates. Be ready."

"I was born ready. After sleep. And coffee. Definitely armed." I patted my holster.

Drago glanced down at my gun hanging in its holster. His gaze slid up, pausing on my cleavage before shooting back to my face. His lips parted, distracting me.

Suddenly, I was possessed by a hot-blooded hussy. I touched the hard muscles of his chest. I didn't even recognize the throaty purr that passed my lips. "Do you wanna come in?"

Drago stilled. He didn't say anything for an interminable moment. I listened to the shallow rush of his breathing and fancied I could hear his heartbeat in the silence. Something odd stretched between us, building the way a summer storm did, boiling and alive.

Finally, he lifted a hand. His knuckles caressed my cheek, leaving a different kind of fire on the same skin that had burned under Callahan's blood.

"Eight a.m. comes early." His husky voice vibrated through my taut body, plucking me like a violin. "I expect I will see you soon. *Behave* tomorrow. Commander Wingroot wishes to find Callahan as much as you do."

His warm fingers fell from my cheek, and he strolled away without a single glance back.

§

EIGHT A.M. *DOES* COME early, especially for a cop used to second watch. Those late nights and even later mornings had spoiled me for existing like a normal person.

It was obvious, however, that I was no longer a 'normal' person. I shoved back the covers and yawned, planting my feet to rough carpet. Sassy blinked from my pillow and closed her eyes again — too early for the cat was much too early for me.

Three steps across my bedroom floor, I noticed the dust. I groaned, shoulders slumping as I stared at my bare feet. This would be hard to explain to my Major, the career-Marine who ran my division with an iron fist.

I set coffee to brew, ensuring I would have enough for Narcissa,

HEATHER MARIE ADKINS

and opened my front door for the paper. My work phone had been blissfully quiet since I arrived home from the hospital. Callahan had been shot, so I doubted he'd be kidnapping again so soon. But I was a glutton for punishment and started every day reading about the media's opinions on law enforcement. It fueled me for yet another night protecting people who didn't give a damn about me.

As I stooped to grab my bundled paper, silver dust billowing from my toes, the door across from mine opened, and Mr. Kresge popped into the hall. He was a willowy man in his sixties, with wild, Einstein-ian hair and arctic eyes that — though kind — never missed much.

I froze mid-bend, sure he would mention the fairy dust. I was already racking my brain for an explanation that didn't include 'athlete's foot' when he remarked, "Lara! Always a pleasure to see you, my dear. It's going to be a fine day!"

I straightened, perplexed.

He locked his door and pocketed the key in his old-fashioned vest. "I'm off for breakfast with my cousin. Old fool can't half remember the date, most days, but he's never late. But you're up early! I hope that means you're taking a well-deserved vacation. Such a nice young lady as you, you're going to work yourself into the grave if you aren't careful. Anyhow, must be off. Do give your mother my best."

I stared after him until his footsteps faded in the stairwell. I glanced at my feet — yep, still dusting enough to frost a damn cake. Mr. Kresge either hadn't noticed or couldn't see it.

This faery thing sure was odd.

§

NARCISSA'S KNOCK CAME PROMPTLY at seven-fifty. Early, as Drago had predicted.

I opened the door, ready to give her my warmest welcome until I registered the distaste on her face.

"Charming building," she said haughtily. "Are you aware there are cockroaches?"

"They always pay rent on time," I responded with a shrug. "Do, please, come in and judge my home, too."

Narcissa passed into my foyer, as out of place as a witch at Catholic mass. She'd either worn the exact same khaki cargos and black polo emblazoned with a gold SEA logo, or she had a closet full of the same uniform. Silver dust spilled from her black boots, reminding me of a fae man whose boots I actually wanted in my home.

Sassy sauntered from the bedroom at the sound of the arriving visitor. Visitors meant treats and pets, and she wasn't quite as prickly as her owner, bless her. But the moment she laid eyes on the commander, my feline partner hissed and ran, her tail fluffing like a bottle brush before she disappeared back into the bedroom.

"Good girl, Sassy," I called after her.

Narcissa pretended not to notice and plowed through my apartment as if she owned the place. "There is trash on your kitchen table."

I shut the front door and eyed my table. "That's my gunbelt, my weapons, and my badge case. I can see how you could mistake it for trash."

"Regardless, I need you to remove the detritus for our training to begin."

I bit the inside of my cheek before I could snap something obscene, like threatening a pox on her house. Instead, I gently cleared the kitchen table of my most prized possessions and opted to *not* offer her a beverage.

I could spar in polite Southern style, thanks to my mama.

"The blood bond is quite simple," Narcissa began, once settled in a chair. "It exists inside you now, a new sensory organ no different than your beating heart. It connects you directly to the fae who turned you."

"If it's so simple, why do I need you?"

Her jaw hardened. "Do tell me, Miss Cromwell, if humans are known to receive new limbs and walk the same day. Or perhaps they require extensive physical therapy to reach that point. Hmm?"

I hated her saucy face. "Then let's get my therapy started because my patience is already wearing thin."

Thus ensued a really long, really trying eight hours I would never get back.

Visualization, meditation, chanting — what the hell was this shit? I was a cop, not a god damned gypsy priestess. I couldn't "visualize the silver thread of my connection" any more than I could spread my arms and fly to fucking Timbuktu. I didn't even understand the words I had to chant, so what good could they do me?

I plowed through the coffee and the rest of my patience by noon, and switched to hard liquor after lunch. And still, she pushed.

"You are not trying hard enough, Miss Cromwell."

"*Concentrate*, Miss Cromwell."

"No, no, don't squint. This isn't a movie, Miss Cromwell."

By the time the sun had begun its descent, I'd reached my limit. If I had to listen to her snap my name in irritation one more time, I'd resort to homicide, lose my badge, and end up back in the Pepto-pink bedroom at my mother's, being chided to pluck my eyebrows regularly.

I grabbed my empty glass and contemplated a refill — rocks, heavy on the whiskey. My head felt woozy, which probably meant I'd reached my limit.

Narcissa spoke before I could decide. "Miss Cromwell, I question whether you understand the seriousness of your position in all of this."

And there was my limit. "Of course I do, you bitchy twat. You've reminded me every moment since you walked through my cheap, plasterboard door."

My anger felt like a pulsing demon inside me. I embraced it — and the drink — and was fully prepared to throw my glass at her perfect steel-gray hair, when the vision hit me.

A dark alley. A tall figure dusting silver on concrete. Laughter from a fenced yard — a family of four enjoying a sprinkler on the summer night.

Callahan watched.

Waited.

I knew where he was.

CHAPTER SEVEN

could have blamed the sudden connection on my inebriation, or on a full day strengthening that 'muscle' between Callahan and me. Ultimately, it was both, I'm sure, coupled with my burning ire toward Narcissa and her dismissiveness. A need to prove myself worthy, just like the need to do so that had shadowed my entire career in law enforcement.

I didn't fail gracefully.

I tore across town in my cruiser — no lights, no sirens — a bat out of hell with my co-pilot hanging on for dear life.

Narcissa clutched the *oh shit* bar above her head, her gunpowder eyes the widest I'd seen them. She smacked the dashboard. "Pedestrian, Miss Cromwell!"

"They'll move." I grinned, not a little pleased my driving scared the crap out of the faery commander. The man crossing the street hopped onto the curb inches before I would have hit him.

She clutched the bar tighter and closed her eyes. "Dear heaven. I so appreciate the lack of vehicles in sidhe."

"No cars? How do you get anywhere?"

Narcissa huffed. "Portals, Miss Cromwell! Keep your gaze on the road ahead!"

I chuckled and reached for the radio. "You wanna call in your back up or mine?"

"Both, I think." She seemed flustered, as if my death-defying driving had erased any recollection of where we were headed and why.

I unhooked the com and made the call into dispatch requesting -*quiet*- back up to my parents' neighborhood. No need to announce the arrival of half of Savannah's finest.

Narcissa hit a button on her lapel, and a small red light began to pulse.

I raised an eyebrow in her direction.

"The road, Miss Cromwell!" she snapped. Once I'd obligingly put my eyes back on the asphalt, she explained, "It's a transmitter. The alarm will sound at headquarters, and my coordinates will be given to responding officers."

"Fancy. Here we just started wearing body cams and hooting over fire." I mimicked the *ooh-ooh-ooh* of a gorilla.

Narcissa sighed.

Luckily, the house Callahan currently stalked was a good distance from my childhood home. I sped past the familiar split-level, thankful my mother hadn't decided on that particular moment to prune her rose bushes. I did *not* need an irritated phone call from her demanding to know why I was not at home recuperating from my concussion and telling me to slow down.

I double-parked beside a white pick up two streets down and cut the engine. As one, Narcissa and I exited the cruiser and palmed our guns. I heard her safety click off a millisecond before mine.

We slid through the darkness in silence. Narcissa moved like me, light footsteps, weight on the balls of her feet, ready to react. I recognized the kindred soul in her, hidden beneath her craggy exterior and fear of human cars. She was just like me: a cop.

We shifted through the dusky evening, turning into the alley behind a row of houses. Callahan's shadow melted into the trees. If I hadn't been in his head and seen through his eyes, it would have been difficult to place him. As it was, I didn't see his outline so much as I saw a shimmer in the air, a hint that an empty space wasn't quite as empty as I thought.

I thought I would have time to concoct a plan. But nothing ever really happens the way we want it to, and in law enforcement, you have to make split-second decisions that could change your life — and other lives — forever.

There was silence in the alley. The family no longer screeched and laughed. But through the slats in the wooden fence, I could see the toddler remained behind in a little sandbox, chubby fingers digging away happily.

Callahan moved.

Narcissa and I didn't need any special signal. We launched as one, moving faster than a human could move. Warm air blasted past my face, my shoes pounding the asphalt so quietly I felt like a ghost. Then we made contact, her bulk taking out his legs and my arms wrapping around his broad shoulders.

The three of us hit the ground hard, Callahan taking the brunt of the force. His head hit the concrete, and his eyes fluttered closed.

Concussed, I hope. Bastard.

He bucked beneath us, long arms flailing. Suddenly, the dangerous glint of a gun sparkled in the moonlight, and a gunshot rang out.

White hot pain ricocheted through me. The bastard had SHOT me. I glanced at my bicep where my blood shone crimson, shocked that the asshole had managed to get that close to killing me. Then I reared back and hit him in the temple with my weapon.

He collapsed to the ground. Out.

Narcissa breathed heavily behind me, her arms on his legs. "Are you all right, Miss Cromwell?"

I felt a twitch in my eye. "For fuck's sake, Narcissa. Call me Lara."

Her responding laughter twinkled like a wind chime.

Law enforcement of both the human and the sidhe kind swarmed from all directions. Carrington offered me a hand up, while a short, stocky faery covered in blue tattoos handcuffed Callahan with cuffs that shone silver in the night — magickal, I was sure.

"You okay, tiger?" my partner asked, clapping me on the back.

I nodded.

"How'd you find him?"

I watched as two faery officers jerked a disoriented Callahan to his feet. "You wouldn't believe me if I told you."

CHAPTER EIGHT

J could admit, at this point, that magick had its perks. All it took was a bit of faery dust and Narcissa's in-charge tone to convince my department that she was the head of a special FBI unit there to take Callahan into custody. The human lieutenant's wary nature turned to acceptance after Drago dusted him from behind like god damn Tinkerbell in army boots.

I stood with my faery godfather across the street, surveying the clean up. Narcissa and a small army of sidhe enforcement officers had disappeared in a black SUV they'd conjured from nowhere, leaving the two of us behind to supervise the humans as they took statements and wrapped things up.

"I'm in the market for a new partner, you know." Drago's velvet tones woke me from my inner musings.

I glanced across the road at Carrington. He stood beside a new officer, gesticulating, speaking animatedly. Teaching the kid. I'd done everything I could for Carrington. He was a great cop; a great friend. He'd been my number two for so long I barely remembered riding the beat before he came along.

Maybe it was time for him to be number one.

"I think I am, too," I responded, grinning at Drago.

He brushed his fingers over the back of my hand. "What about coffee? I'm in the mood for something… sweet. Warm."

Heat flooded me. I willed away the blush and opened my mouth to respond, when my cell rang. Miranda Lambert sang about hidin' your crazy, and I groaned.

"Hey, Mama."

"Lara Mae Cromwell! I just saw you on the news! They say you got shot by some maniac!"

I grimaced and glanced at my arm; honestly, I'd forgotten about the gunshot wound. Blood had dried on my skin, but the flesh had knitted nicely back together.

The best of fairy, I thought.

"Lara, I can't take this any longer. You need to settle down and give me grandchildren and stop all this gallivanting. First, a concussion, then a gunshot wound — in one week! What's next, child? You gonna get dead?" She ended on a hysterical screech that caused even Drago's eyebrow to raise.

I rolled my eyes. "I love you, too, Mama. Chat soon." I hung up the phone and switched it off then caught Drago's eye. "How's the coffee in faery?"

His lips did that damnable quirk. "The best."

"Wanna go now?"

He stepped into my personal space, and I didn't even flinch. One strong arm slid around my waist and he kissed me — chaste right now, but with the promise of much, much more to come.

"Yes," he murmured, lips brushing mine. "Let's go right now."

The human world tilted on its axis, and I rode the waves of energy with Drago into a whole new life.

AUTHOR HEATHER MARIE ADKINS

HEATHER MARIE ADKINS loves magick and words, but not necessarily in that order. She worships the moon and stars, and revels in the feel of grass beneath her bare feet. She is the author of numerous titles including *Abigail* (Witch Faery, Book One); *Mother of All* (Hedgewitch Mysteries, Book One); and *Wiccan Wars*, the first book in an occult bestselling trilogy. Heather lives in north-central Kentucky with the love of her life and a house full of cats.

Find out more about her at heathermarieadkins.com.

If you enjoyed *Fae Touched*, be sure to join her mailing list for chances to win free ebooks!

If you enjoyed *FAE TOUCHED*, check out *THE TEMPLE*

Vale Avari has a mysterious past and a laundry list of super-powers, but that's nothing compared to what she finds upon moving from small town U.S.A to even smaller-town England.

A chance dart throw lands her in Quicksilver, an off-the-map place with a big problem — people are dying, and word is, it's supernatural.

At her new place of employment, a temple dedicated to the ancient Mother Goddess, Vale learns something even more shocking — women guards are disappearing at an alarmingly patterned rate; women who possess special gifts like her own.

Supernatural powers aside, Vale isn't ready to believe in the Wild Hunt as the culprit, and she's determined to prove the deaths are acts of human violence.

Plagued by a brute with a history of domestic violence and lusting after a dark-eyed man with a secret, Vale has a limited amount of time to discover the killer before he strikes again. In the process, she'll learn things aren't always what they seem and the supernatural might not be so extraordinary after all.

The Hunt could ride for her.

Available at Amazon.

FINDING HOME

BRITTANY WHITE

§

"*B*rigid, darling! Will you please come in for dinner? It will get cold!"

I heaved a sigh as Mother's voice called out over the field. Despite her calls, I longed to be a part of the land, instead of merely living on it.

The land held a strange magick to it, a magick that whispered my name in the summer heat and covered me in a winter storm. I reached my hand out toward it, willing the vastness to capture me.

Sadly, I had no power over the elements, no voice to call the creatures of legend, and no amount of prayer could turn me into anything but an average girl. With one last look to the outside world, I walked back to our thatched hut and barred the door with a heavy board.

Mother had a fear of open doors. Ours remained locked at all times. Father didn't dwell on it, but it bothered me to pure distraction. No fool would sleep with an unlocked door, but we lived on the outside edge of our village; we didn't need to fear robbers. We had nothing worth stealing.

I shuffled across the dirt floor of our hut in my bare feet, and rested my elbows defiantly on the table. While most girls would be staying out late into the night to celebrate Alban Heruin, the longest day of the year, I would be imprisoned inside until dawn. The town had picnics on the fields; games they played; and elaborate rituals to please the gods and goddesses. At the end of festival, a huge bonfire would light the way through the darkness until the sun shone the next day. Many girls used this quiet night time to meet their lads and make mischief in the grass.

Mother did not approve of such antics. She didn't like the boys to call on the house, and she never let me out at night.

She noted my pouting, but stood firm in her resolve to keep me shut inside.

"Brigid, every year is the same. Food, games, and fire. You see the children every day in the fields, so I don't know why you seem so desperate to see them tonight. I'll not have my only child make mischief and get herself with a babe before her time. Those village girls ought to

BRITTANY WHITE

be ashamed. Having babies in that fashion. No girl should get married."

My father said nothing, but I saw him raise an eyebrow at this remark. He knew better than to interrupt my mother, but sometimes I could goad him into it.

"I suppose I will follow your example and never marry then."

"Now, Brigid," my father said sternly, "I will not tell you to stay out of the marriage bed, or the birthing bed for that matter, but the boy must be able to care for his babe. Are we clear?"

Mother cut in, the very idea of me being with a boy making her red-faced. "As long as you live with us, you will abide by these rules. We do this for you. To keep you safe from the danger that lurks outside."

I knew wolves prowled the darkness. I had heard rumors of monsters and creatures not of this world, and even tales of child-snatching witches. The wolves I could hear howling in the night, but the other tales only served to scare small children.

"The only danger out there is afraid of fire. No wolf would get me so long as I didn't wander away. I don't see why I can't go. I've seen sixteen summers and have had my bleeding months for three of them. I'm a woman now, Mother. I want to have fun with my friends. I cannot do that if I am locked in my room. Please, let me go! I promise I won't be alone with any boys. I will stay with the women. Please."

My pleas fell on deaf ears. Mother stuck to her word and locked me in my room before nightfall.

I pretended to cry for a time before I got to work on my plan. I had known all along that she would never let me go to the festival. I had been preparing for my escape for weeks now. I crawled under my bed, reaching for the small trowel hidden there. Caked with dirt, the handle wobbling from use, it seemed a pitiful tool, but it achieved its purpose nonetheless. I uncovered the hole beneath my bed and set to work digging the rest of a hole that measured just about my size.

With a little pulling and pushing, I managed to wiggle my way out. I had laid my summer dress just outside and fixed my hair in a loose braid. On the outside of the house, I placed a small piece of thatch to keep the hole hidden. I didn't bother with shoes, racing as fast as I could toward the center of the village.

Music from drums and flutes blared loudly the closer I got. Children danced and made up silly songs, while the adults said more serious prayers. I stayed back from my elders, knowing they would give me up if they saw me. Everyone looked out for the children, and while they didn't agree with it, they respected my mother's wish to keep me inside.

The younger adults would lenient and more likely to keep my escape a secret. They had begun gathering sticks for the bonfire, talking excitedly.

In a moment, I felt overcome with apprehension. The guilt of disobeying my mum weighed heavy on my stomach. I turned to go home when one of the younger children grabbed my hand, pulling me into her group with a toothy smile.

"Ah, so Brigid has finally come to the bonfire." Sochi, the village oracle and healer, had a way of seeing everything.

My stomach dropped. She would tell my mum that I snuck out.

"Well, my mother.... You see, she doesn't know..."

Sochi nodded in understanding. "I had a feeling you would be here tonight. I'm sorry I have not been more vigilant. I could have kept you from the pain."

It takes a village to raise a child, and I had a feeling this child would get a whipping tonight. Hanging my head low, I followed Sochi away from the fire.

"What has gotten into that head of yours? You know your mother will be furious when she finds out you disobeyed her."

"Please, Sochi; I only wanted to join in the fun. I've never gotten to celebrate the night festivals. I'm always locked up, and I hate it. I feel like a prisoner, though I committed no crime. Please, at least tell me why Mother is so protective of me."

Sochi stared at me for a moment, strange thoughts playing across her eyes. She seemed to be debating in her head what words to say.

"Your parents should have been the ones to tell you. However, I doubt it will matter. You will never make it back before the moon rises. Come, take my hand, I will take you home."

Sochi led me back up the path, quiet for the longest time. She seemed to be waiting for something. Slowly, the moon rose high over us, and I gazed in wonder at the round orb. I had never seen the moon before. It looked magnificent, glowing in its pristine beauty. As I stared at it, my skin reflected the illuminating light, shining in the darkness, a beacon brighter than the sun.

The air became chilled. I could see my breath before me. It seemed like a crisp morning frost, instead of the summer heat that I should have felt.

Sochi must have noticed it, too, for she grabbed my arms and pulled me up the hill. I had never seen her so rigid and serious before. It frightened me. Ahead of us, Mother appeared over the hill, her shawl clutched tightly around her body. The chill in the air reminded me of a snowy winter. Sochi met my mother halfway before turning back to the village.

"Brigid, you must run to your mother. Try not to look back. What you see, or don't see, may frighten you. Get to your house, and stay there!"

Standing in the brightness of the moonlight, my mother began to cry.

"Mother, it's all right. Please don't cry. I promise I won't ever leave the house again." I reached forward to calm her. I stopped when I saw my hand glistened almost silver-white in color. It shown like a thousand polished pearls. My hair shone even brighter, as if every star had come to life in its strands. It had also grown several feet, reaching far past my back. I glowed like the moon, and looked to my mother for answers.

Mother fell to her knees, clutching me tightly. "I told you not to go outside. Now they will come for you."

I said nothing as she wept in despair. The summer heat had come back full force, and I began to sweat. A howling on the wind startled me, a morbid blood-curdling sound that froze me to the bones. Hearing the howl, Mother pulled me alongside her, running for the house. I could hear, more than see, the wolves approaching. I could feel their breath, but even the glow from my skin did not illuminate the danger.

Father stood at the door, a club in his hand, ready to fend off the pack. "Freyja, get the girl inside. Stay out of sight!"

"Father, no!"

I could only glimpse his back before he shut the door. Mother bolted it shut behind him. He stayed trapped outside, the only thing standing between us and the wolves. I cried for him loudly, but Mother held me back.

"Mother, we have to let him in! The wolves will eat him alive!"

Mother remained silent and calm as the shouts and scratching echoed around us. They tried to get inside. I clung to her in a way I hadn't done since childhood.

I gasped. "Wait, my room has a hole in the wall. If they find it..."

Silently, she pulled me back towards her room. Pushing the wooden beam down over the bedroom door, she turned to shove aside a rug half-hidden by the bed. A door beneath revealed a tunnel under the house. It frightened me.

Grabbing a small candle, Mum shoved me toward a shaky ladder. "We have to go! Get in the tunnel!"

She climbed down after me and bolted it from underneath, revealing a Celtic knot etched into the wood. Pulling me along a dark path, she urged me to run faster. Would we make it before the wolves got in? My head argued the door had been bolted shut, but my inner voice knew there had to be more.

"Mother, what's going on? How long has this tunnel been here?"

She didn't answer my questions until we neared a large stone wall. The heavy boulders looked hard to move. Beside the stones, a rough hide rested against the rock, tied with thread. Unrolling it, she pulled out a dense black cloak. It looked heavy but felt wispy and cool in my hands, like mist. From inside the cloak fell a lambskin satchel, covered in the same knots I had seen on the latched door.

"Mother, please, talk to me. What is all this stuff? Where is Father?"

"Your father is likely dead, and if you do not hurry, you and I will be next." She grabbed my hand and forced me to kneel with her beside the boulders.

"Listen to me, child. I never meant to lie to you forever. I meant to tell you everything once you had grown. I'm sorry. I should have told you everything. I put us all in danger. It's my fault."

My eyes filled with tears, my brain uncomprehending. I could hear howls, faintly echoing in the tunnel.

They had gotten in.

"Brigid, I don't have much time. Sochi knows all that happened the night you came to us. She will protect you. You must leave this place. Put this robe on, don't take it off. I can give you some time to get away. We are out of time." She rose off the ground, covering me in the black cloak.

"Mother, what are you going to do? What if they catch me?"

"The cloak will hide you. Do not take it off at night. They will be drawn to your glow. Go now." She took my face in her hands, shaking with fear. "I know I shouldn't have kept this from you. Know that we will always love you, no matter what happens."

Kissing my forehead, she pushed me towards the stones, which began to move like magic. The opening allowed me to pass through with ease.

"Do not turn around, Brigid."

I heard the stones move, darkness closing in around me. Running with all my strength, I hoped Sochi could help them. I ignored the silent voice saying *They are not your parents.*

Near Sochi's house, I screamed her name between gasps for air.

"SOCHI! Please... YOU MUST HELP! My mother and father are in trouble."

I slid down the front of the door, my strength nearly gone, and my voice hoarse and dry. The door opened. Sochi put a single finger to her lips and motioned me inside.

"Sochi, you have to help me! My mother... She kept talking... Saying that I'm not her daughter! The wolves came, and... Please help!" I sobbed from exhaustion and fear, the summer heat choking the air from me.

Sochi's eyes studied mine, pity playing clearly across her face. When she spoke, the words sounded soft and carefully chosen. "Brigid, these wolves... Did you see them?"

"No. Not even their eyes. I saw nothing."

Sitting on the floor by her fireside, the warmth came over me and my breath returned to normal. Sochi gave me a drink to cool my body, as tears cascaded evenly over my cheeks. Playing with the ends of my white hair, I marveled at the way it caught the light. Sochi covered my hair with the cloak, and then walked away. She grabbed several wooden Celtic knots, carefully placing them against the doors and windows.

"I told Freyja to keep these knots over her door and windows. She should have listened." Lighting a bundle of sage, she made a sweeping motion with her left hand, starting at the top and continuing until she had formed a perfect star. She repeated the motion once over every entrance.

"These are blessed, by the same faerie whose blood you bear in your veins. Your mother may not have had a chance to tell you the truth. Brigid, you are faerie born."

This news stunned me.

"Sochi, that is not possible. I am a mortal girl. I am normal."

Looking down at my bright hair, the truth began to sink in. Normal girls didn't have hair that changed color.

"She really wasn't my mother, was she?"

Tears soaked my cloak, as the events of the night set in. My parents weren't my real family. I felt betrayed and alone, knowing they had kept this secret and locked me away. Sadness, anger, and frustration burned through me. How dare they pretend to be my parents? Questions I never knew to ask began to form. Who had been my real mother? Why did she leave me? Did she even love me? My emotions swarmed through me in turmoil.

It became too much to hold in.

"They are nothing to me. Those liars! They knew the truth, keeping me locked away from everything. If I had been told the truth, they wouldn't be dead. I am glad they are dead. I hate them! I hate them!"

Grabbing me by the arms, Sochi shook me violently until I stopped screaming.

"Brigid, I know you are angry right now. Believe me, they never meant for you to find out this way. You must know how much they both loved you. You may hate what they did, but I know you don't hate them. Deep down, you know it, too."

Not wanting to hear anymore, I turned to the window, peering into the night. The Celtic knots faced out toward the world. I listened hard for the wolves, only hearing crickets.

"Sochi, I need to know the truth."

She heaved a sigh, tucking my hair further under the cloak.

"Some time ago, your mother, Freyja, wanted a babe of her own. The gods did not bless her with one, taking each child back to the heavens before its first night on earth. Yet, she held out hope. One winter night, a knock came to their door. A faerie woman, small and celestial, begged for shelter for her child. Your mother had pity on her, and let her in."

Sochi refilled my cup with hot cider.

"The faerie woman said that demons attacked her and her people. They wanted to bring the world into darkness. They wanted power. Your mother's people are Moon Guardians. They keep balance with the demons at the darkest hours. They brutally attacked her village, causing the faeries to flee into the night. You were such a small child; I doubted you would remember any of it. Your mother left you in their care, trying to lead the demons away. A small bit of magic hid your true form, so long as you never came in sight of the moon at its highest point. Your own inner magick is at its strongest during that time. Your mother feared that letting you outside, even on a moonless night, would undo the magick. That's why she never allowed you outside."

My foolishness and childishness had cost me my family. They were dead because of me. I should never have left home. Why hadn't Mother told me the truth? If I had known, they might still be alive.

As if reading my thoughts, Sochi put her hands on mine, trying to give comfort.

"Freyja meant to tell you. You mustn't blame yourself. She let herself believe a lie. She made a mistake and paid for it with her life. What's done is done. Now, you must prepare to leave here. You must go find your people, if any still live. If the demons have found you here, they will not stop looking until they destroy you."

Sochi's eyes filled with tears as she held me close to her. Her weathered hands grasped my face, a look of sadness coming over her aged visage.

"You're so young. I'm sorry this is happening to you. After all this time, I had hoped you would be safe here. Something must be changing in the world. The demons would not try this otherwise. Once you find your people, stay with them. Work together. You have strong moon magick inside yourself, but it is not enough to fight them for long."

"Do you know where they are? The faeries, I mean?"

Sochi shook her head sadly. "I only know your birth mother came from the north. If you hope to find them, you must travel in that direction."

I spent the night with Sochi. She prepared food for me, loading the items carefully into my bag. I would travel by day when the demons would be forced beneath the world. At night, my cloak's magick would hide my glowing skin and hair from their sight. There would still be robbers and highway men to look out for, but I shook the negative thoughts from my head. My life had changed forever. Fear could have no place in my heart.

People make mistakes when they let fear take them.

§

THE MORNING MIST CHILLED me. Even in summer, the mornings could freeze a body to the bone. Though close to home, I did not look back, afraid of what could be seen there. I did not want to see my father's body at the front door.

Sochi would spread the word that we had been attacked by ordinary wolves, though I knew the demons had done the killing. They could shapeshift and take whatever shape they wanted.

Past the village, I entered a cluster of trees, sticking close to the highway and hiding in the shadows. Peeling the cloak back from my head, I let the heat of the day wrap around me. I felt like a completely different person from the girl who snuck out of her room just last night. Had it really only been a few hours ago? I felt light-headed, so I found a spot to rest. My stomach growled with hunger, but my provisions seemed small.

I went over my supplies. Even if carefully monitored, the food would not be enough to last the week. Despair set in, and my tears flowed freely. Already my strength began to wane, my limbs and feet scratched and sore. As the heat of the day grew, I felt bemused that I didn't faint under the cloak. Though dark as night in color, it remained light to the touch, nearly floating on my body. There must have been strong magick within it.

Keeping the sun to my right in the morning, I tracked my movement the best I could. All I knew of faeries, I had learned from stories as a child. Their preference for darker glens, dense forests, and any place they could find that offered seclusion from outsiders was not much to go on.

Mid-day, I spotted a small stream, clear liquid rushing over moss-covered rocks. I knelt, a soft prayer of thanks leaving my lips to any god who may have led me here. The water was ice cold, soothing my parched throat. Taking out rations of bread and dried meat, I chewed carefully, savoring the meager meal.

The beauty of the world unfolded around me like a map. The trees provided wonderful shade, the stream added a peaceful sound, and I could see no signs of danger. For the first time in my life, I had freedom. Even if only for a moment, the world had finally stopped and allowed me to breathe. I didn't want to leave that spot, but needed to keep moving. If any of my people survived, I would need their help. I hoped faintly that my birth mother had gotten back to them.

The cloak stayed over my head as the day got hotter. Though tempted to take the cloak off, for comfort, my fear of demons made me cautious. My feet had nothing to protect them from the underbrush that scraped against them. I didn't dare to look for blood. I had nothing to bandage it with. I would continue north, putting as much distance between me and the village as possible.

Only after stumbling to the ground did I assess my injuries. My feet had bled, though not much. Small stones had become embedded in my flesh, and picking these out took more time than anticipated. With the sun dipping low over the mountains, I knew night would be upon me soon. The approaching darkness scared me as I tugged the cloak closer. I would be sleeping outside tonight; not an experience to look forward to.

Though my stomach growled, I held off eating, walking until I found a hollowed tree to sleep in. Praying no creatures found me, I prepared for the long night ahead. Despite my attempt to stay awake, my eyes closed in an intense longing for sleep.

Morning came with a sense of purpose. Light flooded my face, kissing it with warmth and clean air. Though it had been cramped, sleep had rejuvenated me, and the nightmares I expected never came. My energy felt doubled, though hunger pained me from the night before. Taking out my bag, I gasped in surprise to see freshly baked bread and salted meat within. Upon investigation, I found two full loaves, several wedges of cheese, packages of meat and fresh pastries. A fresh change of clothes accompanied by a pair of soft walking shoes lay at the very bottom. I knew these had not been in my bag the day before.

"Perhaps it is a magick bag," I mused.

Deciding not to question it further, and the meal finished, my journey lay before me. It occurred to me I had no knowledge of what to look for. All my hope lay to the north. My family could be there, if I had any left to find.

§

AS THE DAYS DRAGGED on, the weather turned foul. Rain pelted me from all sides, and no shelter could be found once I left the woods. All I had was my bag, which never emptied, the food never spoiling. Starvation, at least, would not be a concern.

My cloak kept me warm at first, until I had to sleep on the ground at night. The water soaked my clothes, though the bag always provided dry ones. Without my cloak, dying from exposure would have been my fate.

I had lost count of the days, looking over my shoulder constantly to avoid travelers. There was no place to hide out here, and my body ached from travel and weariness. In despair, I cried often over the loss of my parents, regretting my words of hatred. No matter their reasons, they had taken me in, raised me as their own. They had loved me, and I missed them. I felt like a lone tree being bent by the unforgiving wind.

BRITTANY WHITE

AFTER A TIME, THE heat returned, light from the sun giving me the courage to pull back the cloak I had not taken off. It felt good to have the warmth of the sun on my face for the first time in perhaps weeks.

Without warning, I heard a fierce holler over the hills. I had been spotted!

My cloak came back up over my head, and my legs raced over the earth. Bandits and murderers frequented the land, and I did not have enough time to hide myself. My cloak hid my light from the demons, but against humans, it offered little protection. I could not take the chance of being captured — or worse. Heart hammering in my chest, I began to perspire. A glance backward proved to be a mistake. A band of robbers on horseback with weapons closed in on me.

There would be no escape!

I knew I could never outrun a horse. I prayed to every goddess and god out there. *Please, let me outrun them! Give me wings! Let the ground swallow me whole.*

Shutting my eyes in fear, I didn't see the rocks and underbrush. As I fell, pain filled my battered body. My knees bled, as did my hands.

I prayed they had mercy and killed me quickly.

"What have we here, then?" A deep voice cut through my fear. Gruff enough to be frightening, but with a softness to it.

Within my very soul, I felt I could trust this man. I was moved to seek out his face, but only a hood — designed to hide the wearer — peered down at me. Muscular arms held tightly to the reins, though he appeared pale. Bits of white hair escaped from under the hood, indicating him to be an older man. The way he carried himself spoke of leadership, with a straight back, broad shoulders, and commanding presence.

"Maiden, I must admit you gave me and my men a good run. Have no fear; we are not here to harm you."

My knees still bled, impeding my attempt to stand.

"I have nothing of value, sir. Please let me go on my way." I felt frightened with his men staring at me. I could guess their thoughts, and it made me shudder.

"Men!"

The commanding sound of his deep voice told them to look away. I hoped that under his command, he wouldn't let them take advantage of me. He reached a hand out to me, but I hesitated to take it. He could still have ill intentions in mind.

"I am Erik. You have my word; neither my men, nor myself will touch you. I swear on my honor." His hand extended again, waiting.

Throwing caution to the wind, I took it. He hauled me up onto the back of his horse in one motion, and led the way back to where I had been spotted.

"I will hear your story, my lady," he told me amicably, "but now we must make camp."

I didn't object and stayed close to him. He worked alongside his men, pitching together crudely made tents. They dug out pits in the dirt and lined them with stones. Filling the pit with dry twigs, blankets, and underbrush made seats. Fires burned low to the ground, cooking meat propped up on sticks. I saw rabbit, birds, and a small hog. Erik sat me down beside a tree, staying close enough that I could hear the conversation. The topic more or less had to do with the dealings of trade. This held no interest for me, so I simply curled up by the tree in my cloak, closing my eyes against my better judgement.

§

I HAD BEEN SO vigilant the last few weeks, but when I awoke, I had not realized how long I slept. Three fires burned in a circle, the men chatting amongst themselves about battles long gone.

Erik gave his word I would be safest in his tent for the night, and while I did not believe him entirely, I didn't want to sleep among the men. He would question me, no doubt, but I would not reveal myself unnecessarily. I knew nothing about my origins; I wanted to discover my secrets on my own. If I did have some sort of power, I wasn't about to let it fall into the wrong hands. A band of thieves would certainly be the wrong hands.

Though Erik had said I would be safe, I did not know how much truth those words held. I had nothing in the way of weaponry, but I felt I could ride a horse. If need be, I would steal one and head toward the north. I felt a sense of panic when I thought about continuing my journey. It caused me great anxiety, and I began to feel the need to rush out of the camp.

Sitting against the wall of the tent, I retrieved my bag from under my cloak. I found the usual portion of dried meat, some bread, and cheese. At the very bottom, I found a dagger made of fine steel, its hilt decorate with precious rubies and emeralds. It felt light in my hand.

This had certainly not been in my bag before. Though I had come to accept the bag held magick, I hadn't any idea how or why it would have given me such a valuable possession. If the men found it, they might kill me to get it. Tucking it back into the bottom of my bag, I finished off the food just as Erik entered. With barely any light and the hood still covering his face, I could not see his features. He carried food in his hand. Had he come to dine with me?

"I thought you might like some food, and perhaps some company," he said, placing a bowl of meat in front of me. I had eaten, but took the offer out of politeness. He didn't have to feed me, so I made an attempt to show thanks.

"Now then." He settled before me. "Tell me your tale, and I will determine if I should help you."

"What makes you think I need help?"

He did not answer, pouring a goblet of ale for me instead. The silence lingered. After it appeared he wouldn't answer my inquiry, I reluctantly began a brief telling of all that happened to me.

"My name is Brigid. I come from a small village south of here. After wolves killed my parents, I sought to find family that may still live in the north. I... I don't know where they may be, or even if they are still alive. I just know I have to keep going. Please... I have nothing worth stealing; I only ask to be left alone. I am sure I can find them if you will only let me go."

My voice shook slightly. I realized he might have considered me a captive, of sorts.

"I assure you, none of us will keep you here against your will. However, I feel you have only told me a half truth. Perhaps there's more to you, perhaps there's not. Regardless, it would be irresponsible of me to allow a young girl to travel alone. I again give you my word, no one shall touch you or cause harm to you here. I put my honor on it."

His words sounded noble, though I remained uncertain. Men needed female companionship. I could not fight them off should they decide to be less-than-honorable in the future. On the other hand, I had no real protection.

"If you...give me your word that none of your men will touch me, then I will stay."

"Very well. We head northwards ourselves to my father's home. We may encounter your kin along the way. Regarding your sleeping arrangements, you will stay in my tent."

My eyes became wide with fear, until he assured me it would be on a separate pile of furs, far from his bed.

"My men follow my command, but I would still prefer you entrust your maiden honor to my protection."

My heart beat rapidly. Could I really put my entire safety into the hands of one outlaw?

"What assurances do I have that you will protect me?" My doubt obviously bothered him, but he stood proud. He never removed his hood, but seemed to be an imposing force, regardless. Fearing he would rescind his offer, I bowed low out of respect. "Forgive me. I had no right to question you."

His gaze seemed to pierce through my cloak. I wondered if he could see me through the blackness.

"You have nothing to apologize for. You know nothing of me. You are a woman traveling alone in the vast wilderness. You don't know who to trust. Believe me, my lady, when I say that I take my vows of honor seriously. A man is only as good as his word. I would sooner fall upon my sword than blacken my name with dishonor. Trust me, or don't. It's up to you."

He returned to the men, giving me some moments of privacy. I fell upon the furs, covering myself in the warmth. I kept the dagger close, ready to use it if I had to.

§

MORNING CAME EARLY FOR me. I had gotten used to waking just when the sun appeared. The camp lay silent, with Erik sleeping soundlessly in his bed. I still had not seen his face, but did not dare move close to him. Reasoning that he had some sort of deformity, for which he felt the need to hide, I knew I had no business looking into the mystery. He offered kindness and protection; I would not betray his trust. Disgusted by my curiosity, I quietly left the tent, intent on washing myself in a nearby stream.

The water had no warmth, but it had been a while since I had bathed. I placed my bag on the ground, searching until I found lavender and other herbs to help freshen myself. For the first time since starting my journey, I removed my protective cloak. Even though I would have been fine in daylight without it, I had been too scared before to remove it. Now, in the morning air, I didn't feel so afraid.

Leaving my outer dress on the edge of the water, I waded in up to my waist. The water froze my pale skin, turning my lips a light blue. I pushed myself further in, washing my hair and body carefully. There could be no greater pleasure than to feel clean. All the stress and fear left me in waves. I allowed myself to sink below the surface, no longer cold.

Surfacing for air, I began to recall memories from my childhood, a life that seemed so far away now. I remembered the feel of my mother's arms around me, my father patting me on the head before going off to work the fields. I missed the smell of fresh baked bread in the morning, the birds calling to me, Mother singing while washing the clothes, and the feeling of being happy.

The pain of knowing I would never see them again hit me hard, as my body sank once more under the water. I could never go home. Sitting under the water, I felt completely alone. I wanted to cry. I wanted my mother.

The need for air compelled me to surface. What's done is done, my only comfort knowing they dwelled with the gods. More light filtered through the trees now. I had taken far longer than I meant to. Making my way to shore, I dressed in dry clothes from my pack, then went back to clean the dress from last night. I held the soft spun cloth in my hands, running my fingers over the light blue dress.

Mother had saved for weeks to go to town and buy the material to make it. I had wanted something really special that I could wear to a neighbor's wedding. She had said she couldn't possibly afford to get me a new dress, and that my old ones would be fine. On the day of the wedding, she laid the dress out for me while I cleaned up. I felt so happy when I saw it. My eyes stung with tears as I touched the dark blue leaf border Mother had carefully sewn into the edges to make it prettier.

"I'm so sorry, Mother. It's my fault. I'd do anything to bring you back." The tears continued, self-pity consuming me. I missed my father and mother so much I couldn't breathe. I kept scrubbing, wondering where my birth mother had gone, if she had made it away from the demons that night, if she still lived. I wondered about my birth father. Had he been a kind man? Did the demons kill him when they attacked the village? Would I ever feel safe again?

Drying my tears, I finished cleaning my dress as best as I could, and laid it out to dry. Suddenly, something hit me from behind. Before I had gained my footing, someone grabbed me. I felt a touch of cold steel to my throat.

"Come now, little lass. Be a good girl. I'm sure you have something of value for me." He forced me to the ground. I knew him to be one of Erik's men, though I didn't know his name. My bag had the dagger in it, though it lay just out of reach. His blade pressed harder into my throat, causing a thin line of blood to run down my neck.

I am going to die. Oh gods, I am going to die!

"You're such a lovely girl. You won't make a sound and get me in trouble with the commander, will you? No, you're a good girl."

"Please, don't...."

I knew this man would have my body if I didn't try to escape. I decided I would rather risk dying trying to get away. He could only hold me down with one arm, while the other still clutched the knife. My free hand came up, flinging dirt into his eyes. He let go of me as he rubbed his face, and I struggled to my feet. I tried to get to my bag, the dagger my only hope of defense. A sharp pain in my arm made me scream. I could see his knife sticking out, blood rushing down my arm.

Just as he managed to drag me back down to the ground, I felt his weight being pulled off of me. Erik stood between us, sword drawn as he threw the man into the stream. Pulling the knife out of my arm, he picked me up by my waist, and held onto me tightly. His voice sounded angry, even threatening, yet his arm held the sword steady.

"You have dishonored yourself. I may yet let you live, if you take yourself away from this camp and never return."

The man growled like an animal, charging at Erik.

"You coward!" the attacker shouted. "You keep the little maiden-head for yourself! Face me in a duel!"

Erik did not immediately respond. He starred at me from under his hood. I could feel his eyes studying my face and delicate skin. When he finally spoke, he sounded deathly calm. It frightened me.

"You have no honor, sir. No duel can give it back to you. Taking a maiden by force, that is the act of a coward. Leave us, and never return." Erik turned his back on the challenger, giving him the opportunity to attack. The man drew his blade, intending to run Erik through while he wasn't looking.

The world stood still, and without thinking, I ran between Erik and the attacker. It never occurred to me that this would be my final act on earth. I only knew Erik was in trouble, and I could save him. Perhaps he would bury me by the water, where the light only just peeked through the green leaves in the summer sun.

The next moment I remember, I sat atop the attacker, my dagger thrust deeply into his sternum. His eyes rolled back in his head, blood seeping out of his mouth and nose. My hand held onto the dagger so tightly, my knuckles looked white as polished bone.

I killed him. I had become a murderer. My body shook with the realization of what I had done. There had to be a punishment for this. Erik would kill me himself. I gasped for air as the thought of death loomed over me, my eyes shifting wildly to where he stood.

Carefully, he stepped towards me, loosening my grip on the weapon. Though stained with blood, the beauty of it did not go unnoticed. He lay it on the ground and unsheathed his own sword, holding its hilt beside mine. The pattern of the jewels seemed identical. It could have been part of a matching set. I didn't dare pick up the dagger, fearing it would look like a threat.

"I didn't mean to kill him, but I had to do something. He lunged for you. You couldn't have turned in time. Please... Don't hurt me. I will go away, far away, if you wish it. Please don't kill me!" I pleaded frantically.

"Where did you get this?" he questioned, holding the dagger out to me.

I could only point to my bag, which I must have gotten to just before the attack on Erik, though I didn't remember grabbing it. Picking it up, he examined it closely, before handing it back to me. Then, to my surprise, he removed his hood, revealing his hidden appearance. I could only stare like a dumb mute.

His hair reached down to the middle of his back, tied crudely with a piece of cloth. His face set with a square jaw, absent of stubble. He seemed more formidable, his white eyes staring into my soul. His skin looked ghostly pale, his hair the color of snow.

"Brigid, you have no idea how long I have been searching for you."

He took a step towards me before falling at my feet, the hem of my dress in his hands. I stood dumb-struck when he began to sob into my dress. I wanted to comfort him, but the awkwardness kept me from doing anything.

"Forgive me. I didn't know."

Before I could ask any questions, his men came from the camp.

"Erik, the cloaked woman is missing and..."

They paused upon seeing the dead man on the ground, a trail of blood flowing into the stream. They must have known I had done it. I only hoped they would be as lenient on me as their leader had been.

"What has happened here?" a man barked.

Erik rose, clearing the tears from his eyes quickly, before addressing them. He relayed the series of events that had unfolded, letting me fill in when needed.

"Then he has lost his honor," the man said. "Let us leave him here to rot. A man with no honor doesn't deserve a proper burial."

There would be no argument; the elements alone would bear witness to his decay.

It felt wrong to leave the body exposed. He would have killed me, but I could not bring myself to begrudge even the lowest man a proper burial. It didn't seem morally right.

"You shouldn't leave him here. Even for what he did, or tried to do, a man needs to be buried. It's the proper thing to do."

My words had no effect. A young boy stepped up beside me, bowing low.

"With all due respect to you and your station, no man who forces a lady deserves a burial."

The men proceeded to drag him from the water, to prevent his blood from continuing to pollute it, before focusing on me. I was not blind to the similarity between Erik and me. We must have come from the same people. One by one, they took a knee, bowing in reverence. I found myself becoming more uncomfortable by the minute. I felt uncomfortable and out of place with this much attention. Fortunately, Erik noticed my agitation, dismissing his men back to the camp. I pulled on his arm, a million questions running through my mind. I opted for what I assumed to be the easiest to answer.

"Tell me how you know me."

"You have many questions. I know this, but I can't answer them here. Let me take you back to the camp."

My agitation had reached its limit. I'd had enough of this cat and mouse game. I'd had enough of being afraid, and I certainly had enough of not knowing anything.

"No!" I said, letting my temper boil over. "I told you everything about me. My whole life unraveled in a single night, the only parents I have ever known, torn to shreds trying to protect me. The only person alive who can give me answers is stone-walling me. I want answers! Now!" I knew I sounded hysterical, my eyes stinging with angry tears.

"Except, you didn't tell me everything, did you, Brigid? You told me wolves killed your parents. It wasn't wolves, it was demons. The same demons that raided our village, and destroyed our people! I know you had reasons for hiding who you are, and you had no reason to trust us, but you could have saved me a hell of a time looking for you, if you had been honest."

Silence hung in the air. He had a valid point. I could have been honest once I realized he wouldn't hurt me.

"How did you know about the demons?"

He stared at me, a look of pain coming over his face. "I know because I lived through the night they came. I saw the demons who burned our village. I watched helplessly when they devoured my father."

My temper receded, my heart aching for him. This man had watched his family die, yet he had shown kindness to me and defended me in my hour of need. I had been wrong to judge him so harshly, labeling him a lawless bandit. I repented of having ever been so unjust.

He did not talk again for several minutes, but I sensed there were some parts of his story he hadn't told me. I waited for him to continue.

"My mother took me and ran in desperation. She entrusted me to the care of a mortal king, who claimed me as his own, raising me to rule. My only sister she took with her."

He had a sister. I dared not hope for what I thought he meant by telling me this.

"I felt a surge of panic one moonlit night. I don't know why I hadn't felt it before, but I knew that my sister needed help. I told the king I would stop at nothing until I had found her, made sure she would be safe. I didn't realize until this morning when I felt your fear that my search had ended. Do you not see it, Brigid? Do you not know who I am? I am your brother."

His arms folded around me, pulling me close to him.

"Forgive me. Forgive for not seeing it sooner."

The news should have surprised me, yet I had a strange feeling that I'd known the truth before he said it. My heart felt light, complete, an unknown pain suddenly healed in a single moment. I had a brother.

Taking his sword and my dagger, he held them up so I could see the hilts.

"These belonged to our father. Mother left me with the sword, you with the dagger. They are for us to protect ourselves and each other, should we ever need to. Brigid, I speak the truth. I am your brother.

Please, believe me. Trust me; let me take you to my home. I can keep you safe there."

The silence lasted only a minute longer before I fell upon my brother's shoulders, sobbing.

No words passed between us. We needed none.

I would go with him to the castle. Perhaps together we could find our kin, our mother, and be together always. All the fear I had endured suddenly lifted from me.

"Let us go, my dear brother. I have had enough of wandering."

He laughed and patted my head. From around his neck, he pulled out a silver amulet. He picked my cloak up from the ground.

"You needn't hide under the cloak any longer. This amulet has more than enough power to protect you. I have one identical to it. It is made from the finest, purest silver. It will hide you from the demons, and guide you to the light."

I felt nearly naked without my cloak, but with each step, I began to feel stronger and braver. We reached the camp to see the men gathering the tents.

"Are we headed back to your father's castle, Lord Erik?"

Helping me onto his horse, he turned to his men, all smiles due to the fortune the day had brought. "Aye, we are going home."

Home.

AUTHOR BRITTANY WHITE

BRITTANY WHITE, the author of *Finding Home: A Brigid Story*, has also participated in a group anthology entitled Jingle Spells. She contributed the story *Molly*. She is a proud Kentucky writer, who is excitedly expecting her first child next year. Through the encouragement of friends, family, and coworkers, her dream is to one day bring a fully chaptered novel to her wonderful readers.

A NOTE FROM BRITTANY:

I would like to dedicate this story to my wonderful fiancé, Jared.

Darling, I love you very much. Your faith in my ability to write
a cohesive story, and your constant support, made it possible for me
to begin the steps to achieving my dream. I know I could not have
done this without your encouragement, and I thank the Gods
every day that we found each other.

Lovingly yours,
One Lucky Girl

TRICKY WISHES

VICTORIA ESCOBAR

CHAPTER ONE

I *wish I remembered this damn definition.*

I lifted my silver eyes from the test paper and stared at my classmate. He ran a hand through his perfect hair, and his pencil tapped the table in an annoying off-beat. I didn't speak to him; I didn't speak to a lot of my classmates on the regular, but there was no way to mistake him for anything but a jock with those arms and shoulders. What he was doing in a sociology class? That seemed a little out of character for someone like him.

Mr. Frederickson's test was unreasonably hard. The professor had it out for us over the boner incident last week. His distress was hilarious to watch, and he had no proof a student dropped Viagra in his glass like he insisted to the Dean, who happened to stop by that day. She was not amused to say the least.

I leaned back in my seat and crossed my Dorothy-red heels as I considered the jock's wish. The fingers of my left hand automatically moved to twist the thick silver chain around my neck as I contemplated. There was nothing about the wish that required a lot of power, and since I would be given the answer as well, there was excellent reason to grant it.

After writing down the definition in question, I snapped my middle finger and thumb on my right hand, jingling my silver and sapphire stone bracelets as I did. The chunky, unpolished sapphire ring I never took off my middle finger twinkled for a heartbeat as my magic flowed out.

Wish granted.

College tests sucked, but if I wanted to stay with the times, I needed to take classes every quarter century or so. Being in college every so often had its perks, too. The huge campuses made anonymity easy for someone with my talents. If my mother ever found out this was how I maintained balance, she'd... Well, I didn't want to think about that.

Besides, giving the hot teacher a boner for a week every time he looked at a female student was amusing. College kids made some interesting wishes. Even after the last sixty years of off-and-on college, these not-quite-adults made for some decent entertainment.

When I turned in my test, Mr. Frederickson accepted it while looking down at his desk. "Have a good day."

"You too, Mr. Frederickson." I smiled as I let myself out of the classroom. The poor man. Maybe a week of hard ons was a little too mean. However, he was a hard ass and had no flexibility for late work, nor did he offer bonus assignments, so at the same time, it seemed fair.

Out in the quad, I stretched and sighed. Two weeks left of this semester. Next semester would be more fun. This one was only boring because of the prerequisites. When I picked my next college, maybe it would be out of country. The US of A was only so big, but the rest of the world... "It's a small world" was a commonplace phrase for a reason.

I ran my hands through my wildly-curled onyx hair and shook it out as I walked toward where I'd left my car. I never made plans, but camping this weekend sounded like the best idea of the week. I needed to stretch in ways I couldn't within city limits. At least, not without getting shot at. In the woods, if I got shot at, killing the man shooting was fair game.

As I settled into my car, I mentally ticked off the list of stuff I needed for camping. Instead of sleeping on the ground, I could rent a cabin, but that would cut into my savings. While money wasn't a problem, being frugal was important. I never wanted money to be a problem. Turning to my father for help was out of the question. Completely.

My puppies would either need a sitter or to come with. They adjusted to my other form well, but were still a little skittish. Some dogs were. There was no changing that.

When I stepped out of my car at my apartment complex, I blew a kiss to the old woman sitting on her patio. Without fail, she was there every day. "Hi, Mrs. Cordry."

"You're a terrible flirt, Lia. What would you do if I ever took you up on that offer?" Mrs. Cordry shook her head and rocked her chair. "You should be more careful with your wishes."

Wishes weren't something I made. Since I couldn't grant my own wishes, there was no point in making them. Wasted breath, my grandmother would say.

There was nothing in the mailbox but junk. The letter from Delphi went into the same stack as the junk. After the first decade, I stopped trying to hide from her. Somehow, even though my mother couldn't find me — thank you gift from dwarves — Delphi always did. At least she found it amusing to keep my location to herself. Though no one, not even a powerful oracle, would cross my mother if it came down to it.

When I unlocked the security door, only its creaking broke the still silence of the building. Not a sound came from any of the apartments as I climbed the stairs and headed up to my fourth floor apartment. The silence was unnatural for this time of day, and I paused a moment trying to listen for some kind of sound. Nothing.

There could be the chance everyone left for whatever task they had planned, but something always made noise in the afternoon in my experience. Even the mice were noiseless. Deciding it low on the importance scale, I continued up to my door and let myself in.

"Nick. Nora. Mommy's home." No scrambling feet greeted me. I frowned. My whippets always rushed me at the door. Usually because they needed to pee.

Having dogs was my favorite mistake. I lived a lot longer than they did. Every time they died, I swore I would never get more. That oath never lasted. Loneliness beat out heartache every time.

In the office off the living room, I set my bag on the chair and glanced briefly at my wall of memories. Photographs of me and the friends I loved covered the wall. Thankfully, I wasn't older than the invention of the camera, but I came close.

"Nick. Nora." I left the office and returned to the real problem at hand. My missing dogs.

A low whine came from the closed bathroom door, and I sighed. They'd shut themselves in again.

"You silly puppies."

A cloth firmly covered my nose and mouth when my hand landed on the door knob. I jolted and struggled to no avail. My assailant was physically stronger than I was. Whatever soaked the cloth made my head spin, and before I could gather my thoughts to use my power, my eyes rolled back. Darkness took over.

CHAPTER TWO

*T*he step team in my temples needed to take a hike off a steep cliff. The throbbing was worse than a night of foolishness with a satyr and hobgoblin for companions. I curled up into the fetal position, a small moan escaping me, and hoped the torture would end.

An impatient tone crept in through the pounding in my head. "Malik, what did you do? You said it would wear off without effects." A man huffed. "Sinbad, I wish the chit awake with no ill effect."

A slight pause followed, and then very quietly, I heard a response. "As you wish."

Something tingled up my spine, and I sighed as the headache abated. Though I was already awake, I felt something flutter against my temples, coaxing my eyes to open. Curiosity forced me to sit up and stretch. The draft of cool air made me freeze and take a quick survey.

Someone had changed my clothes into the tackiest *I Dream of Jeannie* knock-off I could imagine. To make matters worse, my jewelry was gone, and it looked like glass bars separated me from the space beyond.

I didn't care about the clothes, but my silver ring was precious. Brokkr made it, and a gift from the dwarves was not idly lost. In the wrong hands, there would be a lot more grief in the world than I caused with my little pranks. There were things best left untouched, and my ring was on that list of things to play keep away with.

A long-legged man sat in an expensive executive chair staring at me, while another man — dressed like he stepped out of the *Alibaba and the Forty Thieves* musical — stood behind him to his left. There was a bruiser guy on the right and a secretary or assistant-type woman directly behind the chair.

The bruiser likely did the drugging and brought me here. I pondered how to get even. He needed punished for locking my dogs up, as well. My babies were scared piss-less by now. There would be no forgiveness for animal cruelty; he was in the doghouse. That thought made me realize what I could do to avenge my puppies at the opportune moment.

Ali Baba looked like a long-haired, Middle Eastern prince, despite the ridiculous costume. Power leaked from him, but it felt restrained somehow. I wondered what he was.

"So, genie. Let me enlighten you as to your predicament." The seated man stood and strolled over to the bars separating us. "I am Abel Valarius, and I own your lamp, so you obey me now."

I blinked at the Adonis man. He was… stupid. He might as well call me Tinkerbell for how accurate he was in his assumption. Still, fucking with him would be fun. Something was more pressing, however.

"Where's my ring?" I crossed my arms and ignored the extra draft created by the motion. The dangers of dwarven craftsmanship held precedence.

"I wish for infinite wishes, genie." He mirrored my crossed arms and lifted his chin.

Was he for real? Well, I had an easy response for that.

"Have you never seen *Aladdin*?" I rolled my eyes. "You get three wishes. You can't wish for more; I don't bring people back from the dead; and I don't make anyone fall in love with you." I snapped the fingers of my left hand. "Wish denied."

His brows drew together. "What?"

"Should I repeat myself? I don't grant any wish in the universe." I held his frosted emerald gaze when he attempted to stare me down.

"Sinbad." He whirled on the Arabian Nights representative. "You said she was just as powerful as you."

Sinbad dropped to his knees with a startled cry of pain as Abel rounded on him. He clutched his chest and fell completely to the floor as his body twisted with whatever torture Abel imagined on him.

"Believed. I believed her to be as powerful as myself." Sinbad forced the words out between gasping breaths. "She does hold power."

"You have his lamp?" The question was rhetorical. Based on Sinbad's prone position, it was obvious the arrogant fool had the lamp.

Abel turned away from Sinbad and curled his lip at me. "He gave it to me when we were children. To keep it safe."

His fingers twisted the gold chain of a bracelet that looked older than my ring. Sinbad's lamp, I guessed, and then wondered, based on the hammered look of the bracelet, if he was the guy from the stories told about Sinbad and the seven seas.

"You're doing a marvelous job." I made sure my tone was as dry as the desert as I turned my attention back to Abel.

"Don't talk back to me, slave." His voice boomed, but I didn't even flinch.

I lifted a brow and decided it was time to play my game. "You whine like a woman. Do you need some chocolate? Is it that time for you?"

"You arrogant little beast," he roared at me, but I watched the woman standing behind his chair.

If I guessed right, she was here because of seniority within Abel's business. In her professional career with him, she would have seen and dealt with almost everything from him. A woman scorned — or in this case abused — would have a lot of reasons to want to give a little grief back to him.

The secretary rolled her eyes. She did exactly what I predicted a woman in her position would do. *I wish.*

My lips curved into a sharp grin. I didn't even need that much from her, but I had fun fucking with people's heads. I snapped the fingers of my right hand. "Wish granted."

CHAPTER THREE

*T*he secretary's face froze in horror as she realized my implication only seconds before Abel rounded towards my enclosure.

"What?" That was the only word he had time to utter before he collapsed in agonizing pain as his body reformed. Since he was a dick of the worst kind, I made sure the transformation was as painful as possible without him passing out or dying. I wanted him to feel every change.

He laid motionless and silent for several heartbeats before a low moan escaped. The quiet, female cry was music to my ears. He — *she* — groaned again as she pushed herself to a sitting position.

The bruiser whistled. "Damn."

I began laughing. Abel looked ridiculous. Like a child — since his new form appeared to be around sixteen — playing in her daddy's clothes.

"What. The. Fuck." Abel looked down at herself with something beyond horror in her eyes and shoved with irritation at the long, flowing hair. The pressed shirt looked about to burst at the seams thanks to her new cleavage. Maybe triple-D's on a thirty-four inch waist was overkill, but it looked hilarious. The shirt covered her like a dress when she stood, and her pants fell off the narrow waist.

"You bitch." She kicked off the pants, sending too-big shoes across the room. Abel marched to stand directly in front of my enclosure. "Undo it. I wish for you to undo it."

My left fingers snapped. "Wish denied. Now that I have your attention, *Abby*. Where is my ring?"

"I own you." Abel's scream made everyone wince. "You will do as I say." She whirled on Sinbad, moving towards him with purpose. "I wish to be transformed to normal."

I watched Sinbad's curt nod, and a smile formed on my lips when nothing happened. Sinbad's brow furrowed, and he held out his hand to Abel — perhaps to focus — and still nothing happened.

"I don't understand." Sinbad's voice barely reached my ears.

"You pathetic, insolent bastard." Abel struck Sinbad across the face, but considering the new body and height difference, the only impressive thing about it was the sound. "I wish — "

"That's enough. I tire of these games." I didn't really, but Sinbad was an interesting creature who didn't deserve this kind of abuse.

Without my ring, I had no restraints. Nothing stopped me from doing whatever I wanted. Nothing restricted my power. Since it was likely dear, old mommy was already on her way, I might as well go all out.

I snapped my fingers, more out of habit than because I needed to, and touched the bars, shattering them into crystal rain. With some focus, my clothes transformed as I stepped out into the main room.

The tacky genie getup morphed into an elegant black high-low dress that would make any female green with envy. My Dorothy-red heels clicked as I crossed the room to the small group.

The bruiser moved to intercept, and I held my hand out to him with an intent focus. My eyes barely flicked over him. "You're in the dog house. Locking my pets up was your ultimate error."

He cried out as his body convulsed, and the groan of pain turned into a dog's whimper. The little black Chihuahua would never break into anyone else's house again. Maybe poop in their yard; but he had no real power any longer.

The yappy pest raced towards me with jaws snapping. I glared and curled my lip. A low growl from my other half was all it took to make him piss himself before he tucked his tail and cowered behind the secretary.

"Sinbad." Abel ducked behind the genie.

"Tsk." I flicked two fingers at Sinbad and sent him flying into a wall. My eyes, which I knew looked like molten pewter when I was unrestricted, glanced over to the secretary who remained deer-in-headlights still. "Don't interfere."

She swallowed and nodded once.

I grabbed the cowering Abel and lifted her off her feet with one hand. "My ring, little girl."

She pulled off a chain from around her neck. "Here."

The sapphire chunk was warm and familiar when it landed in my hand. Mentally, I exhaled in relief. Protecting it became a full time job some days.

I set Abel back on her feet and held out my hand. "Sinbad's lamp. Hand it over."

"What? No." She backed up, wrapping her hand around the wrist bearing the bracelet.

I sent mental darts at her that dropped her to the ground with a yelp of pain. "Let's make a deal."

Instead of invading Abel's personal space again, I reached for the chair and turned it around. The thing was extremely comfortable to sit in, and I made a mental note to get one for my office. My ankles crossed, and I stared at the cowering girl.

"What kind of deal?" Abel would always be a businessman at heart. Even in the body of a woman. I wish I could witness the effects of her first cycle. The thought made me chuckle.

A low moan crossed the room, and all eyes fell on Sinbad. He tried pushing to his feet but only managed to rise to his knees. Blood, a golden, ichor-looking substance, dripped from his temple.

"Sinbad," Abel whispered, drawing my attention back to her.

"Don't bother. He's too out of focus to grant any wishes at the moment." I replaced the ring on my middle finger and tapped it lightly against the chair. The familiar blanket of restraint returned, and I suppressed a sigh of relief. Control was something I struggled with, which was another reason the gift was important. "So, Abby. I've been around a while; please don't take me for a fool. I know you have to willingly give me Sinbad's lamp for the ownership to transfer."

"I'm not giving you his lamp." Abel pushed to her feet. "Sinbad is mine."

I tilted my head, and my mouth quirked. "His power is nothing to mine, you know. He can't return you to your male form. In fact, I think perhaps it's best for everyone if you learn a little humility and stay in your current form."

"What am I going to do? Everyone knows me as a man." Her face flushed. "I can't go prancing around as a prepubescent child."

"Have you taken a good look at that bust? There's nothing prepubescent about it." My fingers tapped again. "So. My offer. Give me the lamp. Willingly, of course. And I will grant one wish. Any wish but your return to male form or giving you another genie. You've abused that one enough to prove you can't take care of your pets. Perhaps your secretary will take you in and teach you what it's like to be a woman. Though, with that appearance, you'll probably have to go back to high school."

"High school," Abel shrieked. "Are you out of your mind?"

I rolled a shoulder dismissing her question. "Your second option isn't so nice. I take the lamp and destroy it — making Sinbad mortal in the process — and you get nothing. Oh, and you *still* remain a woman."

Silence reigned for a full minute before Abel fumbled with the clasp of the ridiculously old bracelet. "Any wish, you said."

"Except for being a man and another genie." I held out my hand.

Abel sighed and studied the antique hammered metal a moment before dropping it into my palm.

"That's a good girl. Now." I clasped the bracelet around my naked wrist. "What do you wish for?"

"You want it right now?"

"Obviously. I have places to be and things to do. What's your wish?"

"I...don't know. I need a moment to think." Abel unconsciously pulled on her hair.

I tapped a foot, deliberately pressing. "I haven't got all day. I have finals this week, in case you didn't know. I've got studying to do."

"Don't rush me. You've given me very little time. This is an important wish."

"I don't have all day. And I'm not willing to give you all day. Hurry it up."

"Shut up. Shut up. I'm thinking."

Used to her tantrums already, I didn't even flinch at her screaming. "Let's go, little girl."

"Shut up. I wish you'd shut up a moment." Her hands slapped over her mouth, and I grinned. "Wait. You can't. You did that on purpose," she cried when my fingers snapped.

CHAPTER FOUR

The park was full of noise and happiness. After the emotional drain of captivity, and then the power usage, I needed simple pleasures. I accepted the ice cream cone when Sinbad held it out.

"Seemed appropriate." He didn't look at me but out over the park. "What now, mistress?"

The single word was a reminder of the unfinished business I had left. The hammered bracelet was a heavy weight I didn't want permanently on my wrist. I already had burdens.

I spoke without taking my eyes from the squealing children. "Sinbad, I wish your lamp held no power over you."

"What?" His incredulous tone drew my gaze to his face. He was slack-jawed and wide eyed.

"Should I repeat it then? I wish your lamp held no power over you." To emphasize the point, I removed the bracelet and dropped it into his lap. "You are as free as any genie can get."

"As you wish." He fingered his albatross. "He was a bright child. He could have been so much more."

"Power changes the threads of the fabric. You should know this better than most."

"Yes." Sinbad sighed but didn't lift his gaze from the bracelet.

My taste for the ice cream gone, I stood.

"Wait." Sinbad grabbed my arm before I stepped out of range. "I owe you a boon for freeing me."

"Boons are what got you into your predicament, wasn't it? How were you turned into a genie anyway?"

"Ah, well." He rubbed the back of his neck. "There was this thing with Eris, which led to a misunderstanding with the Indian deva...I never did get her name..."

I resisted the sudden urge to rub my temples. "You screwed a couple of goddesses from several pantheons, and they collectively cursed you, I take it."

"You know, it sounds really negative when you say it like that."

"Daughter," an over-exuberant voice called.

I winced, and my shoulders automatically hunched. "Fucking great."

"My precious girl. You don't call. You don't write. What is a mother supposed to think?"

"In your case, Queen Morgause, I would hope you thought I lived my life as I am meant to." I finally turned and faced the Queen of Air and Darkness, the sole leader of the Unseelie Court.

I wish I didn't find her beautiful or alluring. That was her gift and her trap. Sirens weren't as dangerous as the Unseelie ruler.

My mother knew she was beautiful. If anyone challenged it...there was only one to my knowledge that could. Titania, Queen of Song and Light, had power enough to stand up to Morgause and challenge her authority.

Morgause reached out and dropped a hand on each of my shoulders. "By granting pitiful wishes and denying yourself your birthright? My dear girl, when are you going to realize no matter where you run to, you will never be able to run from what flows through your veins."

"I don't run from me." Stupidly, I met her gaze. "I want — deserve — to live however I choose."

"I've allowed you to squander long enough. It's time to come home." Her eyes swirled in shades of darkness that could swallow a soul if she wanted to.

"Lia." Sinbad's hand squeezed mine, and I snapped out of my mother's lure. "We have places to be." Sinbad wasn't looking at my mother, so he didn't see her frown.

"Yes. You're right. I'm sorry, Mother. I have previous engagements. Maybe for the holidays." I turned away from her and tried to control the shaking. In the end, I had to link my arm through Sinbad's and lean on him as he guided us away.

"You play a dangerous game, boy. Your goddess may be put out to find you off your leash."

Sinbad didn't hesitate in his steps. "It was a pleasure meeting you, Your Grace. Do say hello to Eris for me whence you see her next."

I waited for us to be sufficiently away without my mother following. "Aren't you frightened?"

"Of Eris? No. Gods and goddesses have rules to follow, and they're not as powerful as they once were." Sinbad patted my hand in his elbow. "Your mother, on the other hand... People still believe in the fairies. That gives them more power than a long-forgotten pantheon."

"I'm aware of my mother's strength."

"Your strength, too. That's why I couldn't, even as an all-powerful genie, trump your transformation."

"I'll tell you a secret. He didn't actually want to be changed back and that made all the difference." I smiled to myself when he said nothing.

"You were generous with the second wish." Sinbad's hold tightened when I stumbled.

"Aging a form is a small matter." I shrugged. "Where are we going?"

"Nowhere in particular."

"All right." My jaw cracked as I suppressed a yawn. "As long as there's a bed there."

"As you wish, Princess. As you wish."

The End.

AUTHOR VICTORIA ESCOBAR

VICTORIA ESCOBAR writes fiction from her current home in Louisville. She writes whatever comes to mind and because of such has a variety of genres written including Young Adult, New Adult, Paranormal, Urban Fantasy, and Contemporary Fiction. She enjoys staying busy, but most of all enjoys staying creative.

Find her on the web: facebook.com/V.Escobar.Writes

If you enjoyed *TRICKY WISHES*, check out *UNPRETTY*

Being plain and average would be a step up for Sidonie. The book nerd, gamer geek with larger than average jeans doesn't really fit in anywhere. Add a drunk father and a dump in the projects and she's pretty much guaranteed to be a social pariah. There would never be a happily after in her future, unless her books counted. Instead, she has accepted her lot and surrounded herself with friends who genuinely love and support her.

Music. Art. Creating. That's what made Sidonie remarkable. As she began to find a chance of happiness in her gifts, dark forces start to impact her future. A magical world she had no idea even existed could alter the course of her life forever—if it didn't cut it short entirely.

Available at Amazon.

ETHEREAL

K. LASLIE

PROLOGUE

The absence of everything should be nothing. There was no light, sound, nor sustenance in Aaru. Yet we existed. Our civilizations did not thrive by any means, and in reality, our strength weakened slowly the longer the connection to Eorpe was severed. Ironic, that. 'In reality' while we were stranded deep outside the realms of reality.

A few races escaped Eorpe that were not connected to the Mother as we elves were. The strain this heavenly plane exacted upon us did not seem to affect them in the same manner. In fact, some seemed to be gaining strength the longer they were away, while others had simply adapted. No matter the caste, we elves were by far affected the most negatively.

If my recollection of time held true, this day would be the summer solstice. The powers of my clan would be at their peak, our northern brethren at their weakest, and yet we had given up the battles between us millennia before. Peace had been found between the two clans, Wood and Snow, as a symbiotic relationship formed, and we protected one another. Elves no longer fought elves, but defended and partnered against Dwarves, Orcs, and such evil beings that would raid our villages.

Then came Man. What danger could a non-magical, infantile race be to the great races? They had no spiritual connection to Eorpe. They forsake her, thinking they knew what was best for themselves. The Dwarves called them weak, the Orcs named them ignorant, we christened them lost. Despite the downfalls of Man, they had one thing we did not: Numbers.

The individual lives of Man had always been short, a mere blink of an eye to the rest of us. The early years that shaped an elf were but half over when a man's existence was snuffed. However, in those short lifetimes, they procreated more rapidly than the hare, quickly covering Mother Eorpe and pushing the great races into hiding. The diseases they carried spread like the seeds of a dandelion floating on the wind. Cures were accessible to them, right beneath their very feet, in the fauna surrounding them, yet they were too ignorant to see.

I was the lone survivor on the final expedition to meet with Man on a summer solstice long ago. For centuries, we hid in any remote location we could find. The races quickly learned to set aside our differences and join forces against Man. The most unsettling feeling I ever experienced was the day I entered a Dwarven keep, the rock surrounding me as if I were being buried alive. I knew the rock was made of the Mother, yet the air was musty and stale. I recognized that the rock was strong and stout, yet I was accustomed to the give of a bough in the wind. I left my people within the keep to search for an escape as I led a group on one final attempt to make peace with the curse of our race: the destroyer of our Goddess, Mankind.

The group was small. We couldn't afford the risk of losing more people, nor did we want to seem a threat. I was the youngest elf on the Council at the time, eight hundred and seventy two, yet they chose to follow me. A stout dwarf — Zagaat, as short tempered as he was broad — stood beside me as a show of strength. The orcs chose to send their greatest healer, En'Sheer, as a show of peace. His body was encrusted with mold and fungus, a mottled camouflage of medicinal powers always within reach. A forgiving giant, Gestar, came as a sign of hope. He was the last of his family, which he held sacred almost to the level of the Mother herself. Yet he directed no hate toward man, this tribe the very one that took everything away from him.

Regardless of our peaceful intentions, fear overcame the village of men. They screamed of magic, yet I was the only one of our group accomplished in the arts, and I avoided casting even a spell of calm to avoid such a calamity. Perhaps if I had attempted more, I would not have been the only to return. We abandoned all of our weapons; they surrounded us, shoving spears in our faces. There was no reasoning to be had with them as they corralled our group of four to the central square. An elderly woman — her apron stained with blood, carrying a headless chicken in one hand and a knife in the other — hobbled out of a doorway in great pain. She pointed the knife at us, rambling some sort of nonsense I was unable to decipher over the murmur of the gathering crowd.

En'Sheer offered assistance to her, a way to remove some level of the pain, to give her mobility back to her. He slowly lowered his hands and removed a tuft of mold from his thigh and a pinch of fungus from his elbow, then carefully ground them into each other in the palm of his hand. He reached out to her with the mixture. But the young man beside her, not more than a child, chose to ignore the offering as help. His fear overtook all rational thought. More quickly than anyone could react, his spear gutted En'Sheer in one fluid motion, the point ripping through the orc as if he weren't there at all.

Zagaat grasped the blade, ignoring the pain as it cut through his skin, and pulled it free of the hands holding it. Adjusting his grip to the haft of the spear, En'Sheer's blood and entrails mixing with his own blood, he spun and freed it from his comrade. He took a defensive stance; the fear of the village could be tasted upon the air. I gathered the energies of the Mother, ready to protect myself in a breath's notice.

Gestar stepped between the furious dwarf and the oncoming horde of man. With his back turned to the crowd, he pleaded for Zagaat to lower the weapon.

A young child seeking to prove himself to his elders slipped through the multitude of men and sliced the giant's hamstrings. He shouted as a man pulled him to safety, 'Let me have my revenge. He killed my mother and father. Let me finish him.'

The weapon in Zagaat's hands became a flurry. His stout frame held strong as he spun the blade in circles, slicing through everyone in his path. I attempted to save Gestar; however, the bloodlust of Man was quicker than my ability to enshroud him with protection. I let the wind carry me away, floating off to a safe distance as I cast a spell of flight. Spears were hurled in my direction, but the winds that carried me also protected me. I watched as my three companions were cut to shreds,

Zagaat the only one able to defend himself, and defend himself he did, until his final breath gave way.

"This is why I have searched you out." My voice rings through the chamber. "Your existence has been known since the beginning days of our time in Aaru. You hide in the shadows of the shadows, yet I wish to bring you into the light. Our time in hiding is over; we must return. Some grow stronger on this plane, yet most are weakening. Let that strength carry us home so that we may exact our revenge on Man. Time has come for man to kneel to the great races as they should have in the beginning.

"I, AigWist, Head of the Council, come to you in a time of need. Assist me in returning our peoples to Eorpe. Together, the Faction and the Council can conquer Man."

A hushed jumble of voices mingled together with urgency in the small chamber. Moments later, as the volume began to grow, a staff that didn't exist tapped a floor that was not there three times. The crowd hushed as a deep voice resonated through the space. "Leave us to speak of your desires. Speak to no one of your time here, or your head will be all that sits on the Council."

CHAPTER ONE

*L*ife existed in Aaru, but in a way no one imagined when they escaped the physical plane of Eorpe. We had no bodies as we floated through space and time, yet we existed with an ethereal projection. The length of my hair mysteriously tickled the nape of my neck. Other elves chose to let their hair grow long, but due to the amount of time I spent with the other races in training, I had adapted many ideals that were frowned upon by my race.

The difference between having a physical body to experience the senses and solely having the capability to do so only in our mind has never been clear to me. Being of the generation born immediately before the escape to Aaru, I have no memories of a true body. My birth was mere moments before the transition. In fact, I was swaddled and carried through the portal without the chance to be cleansed as Man was starting to attack.

The Elders would be furious if they knew the number of times I had observed them talking of their youth and the memories that they struggle to maintain a connection with. The wonders of a rising sun to brighten the day, colors among the sky that could make one weep with beauty, or the Mother's tears falling from the sky. All things were lost to me. The grief that laced their voices as they attempted to make real the experience once again both saddened and delighted me.

The pain they felt depressed me, knowing that what they forgot, I would never enjoy. However, it was just as well I would never enjoy the feel of grass tickling my bare feet while I strolled hand in hand through a dew-soaked field with my love; I would never have the pain of the experience being ripped away from me slowly throughout eternity.

My mind imagined a bow in my hand, an arrow at rest along the string. The bow troubled me the least, yet I had far from mastered any weapon. My instructors varied greatly, from Elves to Orcs, Dwarves to Giants, and weapons masters to magic-wielding savants. No matter my determination or the subject, I had failed. The litany of swearing that had been thrown at me was as endless as the plane we existed in. The shortened version would be, "TaeKuz, there must be something that you are capable of doing; you must only find it within yourself and embrace your power."

My grandfather would be expecting me soon. There was no true privacy in a space where all things are created with thought, vanishing as quickly as the passing of your concentration. The races had adapted to such by discovering how to reach out and feel if the other was willing for your presence to share in their time.

A sensation pulled at my mind, alerting me to his request for my presence. I released the mental grasp my fingers had on the arrow and symbolically watched it fly toward the target, struggling to keep my concentration on the task at hand, straining to keep the flight true. My grandfather's urgency intensified immediately before the arrow's impact, causing my concentration to falter. I lost focus. What would have been a hit on the target became a miss as both arrow and target vanished.

My fingers opened, and I let the bow fall, dissolving toward the ground, before I traveled to my grandfather.

He sensed my disdain immediately. "Grandson, what bothers you on such a special day?"

"Forgive me, Grandfather. I was practicing with the bow, and you know how it troubles me so. I was nearly able to hit the target, but my concentration faltered once again." I dared not explain that *he* was the cause of my distraction, but the anger in my voice certainly hinted at the hidden fact.

"TaeKuz, you cannot let things like this bother you. Your skill will find you when the time is right. I have seen you leading all of our peoples." He reached out to me, and as I stepped near him, he wrapped his arm around my shoulders in a gesture that held comfort from a distant past despite our lack of physicality to feel the other's touch. "Today is a day for celebration, or at least it was in the past.

"Despite our distance and separation, I can still feel the power holding true to this day. In mere minutes, the sun will rise to its peak over our home. Emerald blades of grass will stretch for the warmth of the sun. Our energies will peak before they return to flow towards our brethren in the north.

"Maidens once frolicked through the fields. Warriors sparred in tournament, and families bonded as they watched the festivities. Youngling males found sticks to spar with, while females threw flowers to the winner of the mock battles. We all were fed by the energies, powerful beyond imagination, an ecstasy like no other, for the moments the solstice ruled the sky."

Grandfather shared this same lecture with me year after year. The joy on his face as he would reminisce was the most powerful emotion I had experienced in my life. This was the reason I had started to sneak around and listen to stories of old. I yearned for more of a connection to the Mother.

This year was different than the other five hundred and twenty-one dictations of his memory. His normal explanation of continued festivities was cut short as his eyes closed on his joy and reopened with grief.

"The warmth that flowed through our veins would melt the ice cold of this void. Yet all these years have slowly taken away from us what we thought we were preserving. Our people have become weak and ignorant. Complacency has set in, and most have not noticed that our traditions slip further away with each passing moment. I have spoken with others in the Races, and they suffer from the same dilemma."

"Grandfather, this is a concern for the Council. Why do you speak of such things with me? You know the repercussions would be irrevocable, no matter your station."

The smile on his face was warm and endearing. My fears slowly dissipated as he attempted to reassure me. "Grandson, there are powers in play that are much more powerful than my position on the Council. The façade that we display simply lets everyone believe that there is order in this vacuum we fill. We allow the races to believe there is peace and order. In reality, there is no peace, nor war. No order or chaos. There is the void of space. I am unsure if time even exists as it should."

"Grandfather, please do not talk like this. Are you feeling ill? I should speak to Father. He may know of something to help you through this difficult time. Perchance, would you share your memories of Eorpe? They always appear to brighten your spirits."

His mask of peace vanished as quickly as it had appeared. Vehemently, with such acidity that I had never experienced even from the Dwarven instructors upset with my shortcomings, my grandfather scolded me harshly. "TaeKuz, I forbid you to speak of this conversation with anyone other than myself. We will revisit the importance of it at a later date, but until that time, you are to keep your silence. If I hear the merest whisper of this conversation, I will bring the full might of the Council down upon your head."

Without even giving me the opportunity to respond, my grandfather vanished. The Elves have always been of cool temperament, so to see my grandfather so upset was uncharacteristic, to say the least. I feared that his words held more truth than I was willing to admit, and that frightened me. We were no longer the races we were when we entered Aaru. How would we find our way back to the people that the Mother had created us to be?

CHAPTER TWO

*M*y grandfather's distress continued to eat away at me for some time. Due to the celebrations, I had an excuse to avoid the various trainings expected of me. Most would savor losing themselves in the maelstrom of swords and axes spinning in an artistic rendition of battle, or practicing the alteration of reality by tapping into the magical essence within them.

The art of spellcasting evaded me. In this reality, there was no need to tap into that well within to conjure things. The essence swirled within me, buried beneath a lid that only trickled access. Masters spent decades attempting to open me to the power, on their own or by endeavoring to make me push through the seal that confounded them. I often succeeded in the end result they desired; however, I failed to use the arts. In this plane, anything was possible, or so it seemed until I tried to tap into the power. Due to the fact that our power came from the Mother, the consensus was finally reached that I had not been given enough access to her in the few moments between my birth and our escape.

My parents' lineage was the stuff of legends. Father hailed from a line full of Masters of the Arts as far as our histories take us. I am graced with ancestors that were some of the most powerful in the history of Elves, with my grandfather being the greatest seer of all the races.

My mother descends from a line of the most battle-hardened warriors of Eorpe. Despite the fact that our race was peaceful, there were the elite few who were trained for more than our simple defense. Raids were still required, assassinations to be made in the middle of the night, and multitudes of other activities of which most elves would never know.

My mother's birth was a bit of a disgrace; her parents had expected a great and powerful son. I never understood the reasoning behind the seclusion of women in battle, but perhaps that came from my time training with the Dwarves, where women fought beside men without hesitation. When my father's eligibility as a bachelor was announced, the Council of Elders collaborated and forced them together in an attempt at birthing a battle mage to become legend. Needless to say, I have been nothing but a disappointment — a constant reminder of my mother's shame on her line.

The forms and movements for all of the various weapons flowed through my mind on a daily basis. Spells spilled from my lips in my sleep nearly every night. Unfortunately, *knowing* the motions and incantations does not make one a warrior or mage. This brought much disgrace and shame to my family, to the point that my mother failed to acknowledge my existence.

The void where we resided was empty to all, but many of the elders could fill the emptiness with memories. I, on the other hand, knew of no other existence. All items I conjured through my imagination were based off descriptions from others. While they would meditate, watching the sun rise, the moon travel across the skies, or waves crash on the shore, I chose the enveloping darkness that surrounded us to find peace.

When I distanced myself from the noise of recollection, of creating items and surroundings, only then could I feel the power. There was a pull on me, gently tugging at me, but only I seemed to feel it. Today, the pull was stronger, more of a shove than a nudge, but I had no inclination of where the sensations came from or what they wanted me to do.

CHAPTER THREE

*T*ime had escaped me. I pulled myself from the trance. The shoving had become more insistent, filling me with a power that lingered in my every heartbeat. A new power I'd never felt before that seemed to strengthen my muscles, neurons in my mind firing faster, tendons becoming more flexible.

Thinking of my grandfather brought both peace and unsettled nausea to my stomach. Unsure why, I knew that what he wanted was for the best, even if his approach was strained with unnecessary risks. Speaking with him again was of the utmost importance.

Certain that he would probably still harbor ill thoughts regarding our time together the day before, I chose to attempt finding him without reaching out directly. When his presence began to strengthen in my search, I could discern that he was not alone. They were not energies that were familiar to me, but they stank of negativity. Certainly, they were not the type of people my grandfather normally associated with. He must have been sent on some task by the Council to settle some matter of great import.

Fearing that I would be discovered, I remained at a safe distance and waited for their meeting to conclude. I admit to curiosity over what manner of business they argued — as I could hear muffled exchanges — but I knew that Council business was none of my concern. My grandfather's displeasure would be miniscule in comparison to the punishment the Council would place on one such as myself for interfering with their plans.

The debate continued for nearly an hour before the others involved vanished. No one noticed my presence, including my grandfather, who now looked very disheveled. I searched to ensure that no one was near as I stepped out of my hiding spot, startling him greatly in the process.

"TaeKuz, what are you doing here? How long have you been lurking in the shadows?"

"Well, Grandfather, my entire life nearly. After all, Aaru is nothing but a giant shadow, wouldn't you say?" I tried to force a humorous smile to my face to lighten the mood and hoped for the best.

A small chuckle escaped his lips, but I was unsure if it was genuine. "So it is, young one, so it is. Why have you sought me out? I have much to do."

"Grandfather, I found myself distraught yesterday after our conversation. I sought peace and clarity in meditation, however I was met with the oddest experience. The presence I feel in the void was stronger. Still subtle, but stronger than in the past. When I awoke this morning, I felt different."

"Young one, what were you doing in a trance for that long? You should be careful; that isn't safe." The look of concern on his face changed to inquisitiveness. "How do you mean different? Have you tried any magic? Perhaps you are finally coming into your power."

"No, Grandfather. Not in that way. My body feels different. I feel more agile, faster, and stronger. My thoughts are clearer, but no, I don't feel any more open to the essence within me. If anything, I feel that it is more distant.

"I'm concerned, so I came to you for wisdom. What do you think could be happening to me? I feel as if something is moving me in a direction, but I'm unsure what that direction is. I felt that it was connected to you, so I came to ask for counsel.

"The men you were talking to. They felt wrong, but connected to this feeling in some way. Tell me, Grandfather: what were you discussing?"

My grandfather's expression became stone as he attempted to bury his frustration and concern. He scanned the area for any presence that may have been nearby before taking my hand in his. "Release your hold on this place. Focus solely on me and release all other thoughts. Close your eyes."

CHAPTER FOUR

*O*pening my eyes, I focused on the cool breeze brushing my skin. The surrounding area was dim, candles burning in a circle around me. Someone sat across from me, yet I was unsure who. Their face — and any other distinguishing characteristics — were hidden within their cowl and robe.

The candles flickered before bolting upright and growing in size. Shadows hiding the stranger's face began to retreat in the light. The eyes staring back at me looked eerily like my own, despite a hint of age that betrayed the youth of his face.

"Fear not, TaeKuz. It is I. I have often told you that your appearance to my youth is striking. Perhaps now you can see the resemblance."

"Grandfather, what is going on? Where are we?"

A smirk spread across his lips. "I have brought you into my mind, the only place I can be assured that we are safe to discuss matters without interference from others."

Shock ran down my spine. This was a forbidden art, one of the most sacred rules set up by the Council once established in Aaru. Soon after the transition, it was discovered how easily one could inhabit another's mind. The consequences ranged from fatal to insanity, with several possibilities in between.

"Grandfather, you must let me out. If the Council were to discover what you have done, we would both be punished. You would lose your seat on the Council." Panic started to set in as I attempted to find a way out.

Reaching across the small circle, my grandfather's hand rested on mine. "Calm yourself. The Council forbids this for those that are not practiced. You are safe.

"I fear that I must tell you more than you want to know. I regret pulling you into the schemes of an old elf such as myself, but alas, I am too old to act on my own."

"What do you mean? Who were those men? What schemes?"

"TaeKuz, I have seen the future of our people. If we continue as we are, we will cease to exist. Mother Eorpe is dying. Her strength wavers as man continues to desecrate her. We must return. You must lead us."

I felt a sudden surge in the power as he mentioned returning to the Mother. I could not deny the fact that she was in need of our protection, but how was I going to lead? "Grandfather, I have no skills to lead. I have trained with every race, and they all look down on me. How will I lead? Better yet, how will we return?"

The candles became blinding as they grew to surround us in a solid ring of fire. "I can feel the power you spoke of. The tugging that you feel, that is the Mother. I had forgotten how sweet her presence tasted on my lips as I draw breath given to us from her children. Or how strong the roots of our ancestors support us. How are you accessing her gifts from this plane?"

Grandfather became irate, jealous of the access I had. There were no barriers when sharing your mind with someone else, one of the other dangers in doing so. I could feel every ounce of frustration and rage as he sought to bind me to him permanently. "Please stop. I did not know where the power came from. I had nothing to compare it to."

I could feel a squeezing on my mind as he placed bindings to hold my will to his. "Grandfather, please. I will do whatever you ask. You want to go back. Tell me what I must do. Anything in my power, I will return our people to Eorpe so that we all may rejoice in the comfort of the Mother."

The bindings loosened slowly, but I could feel his strain to keep them. The iron shackles shattered as I struggled to resist. His reluctance was palpable, his desire still strong, but he fought for control. I could feel a darkness welling up in the corners of the space we occupied. A darkness as deep as Aaru, void of everything that we embodied. Frost crept across the floor, spreading up the candles and snuffing the flames.

As darkness encompassed the two of us once again, I heard him reply. "I will find the way to return. You will be placed in the position to lead. Accept the power that is given to you, and do not question. Your role has been foretold, and they will accept my vision."

CHAPTER FIVE

*M*onths passed, and the presence of the Mother slowly dissipated, making me irritable at the loss. Grandfather had been furious, insisting that I was jealously keeping it to myself. He demanded access to my mind to validate the truth. The disappointment on his face was only slightly more noticeable than the nerves that resulted. There was something going on beyond what I was aware, and much to my dissatisfaction I was trapped in the middle of it all.

If there was one thing that my grandfather had been correct about, it was the fact that others would look to me for leadership. My centuries spent fumbling along under the tutelage of masters meant nothing now. Somehow, they all looked to me. Even though I was unable to perform in the manner they all spent countless years instructing me, I knew each of their strengths and weaknesses.

Realization set in that I was the best person to control the mixed forces of all the Races, and the pride I felt was awe inspiring. Even I couldn't believe the power I held. Certainly others would know that despite centuries of peace within Aaru, and learning to exist alongside the other, that Elves and Dwarves did not always work well together. The small nuances of Ice Dwarves having a history of raiding the Snow Elves meant that they should be paired closer to the Wood Elves that had less history of conflict. The pairings became more complicated from there, such as trying to find someone willing to work with the Cyclops and attempt to keep them in line. All of my training over the years suddenly was no longer a failure, but the greatest accomplishment I could have made.

At times, I felt the symptoms of withdrawal once the Mother was gone. There was no comparison to the way everyone else must have felt when they made the transition — the access they'd had their entire lives cut off so suddenly. Grandfather and I could only assume that the pulse in power had come from the Summer Solstice.

We were nearing the second Blood Moon of a tetrad leading to a solar eclipse. From what I was able to gather — by bits and pieces overheard from Grandfather — these were key to weakening the lock that held us in Aaru. With each Blood Moon, the veil would open slightly. The hope was that we would be able to first communicate with some of the Races who stayed behind to gain intelligence. Eventually, we hoped to slip a few of our elite back to Eorpe to allow us time to prepare the proper supplies. Weapons would need forged, food and medicines grown, as well as shelters constructed. All while staying undiscovered. The largest question at the time was if I would lead the exhibition team, cut off from communication with Aaru for months until the next Blood Moon, or if I would stay to prepare the entirety for the return.

Several pushed for me to return, my grandfather amongst the strongest of supporters. The anticipation of being connected with the Mother once again was enticing; however, I was undecided on the matter. The more I was pushed in that direction, the more I felt uncomfortable about being among the first to return. Each moment I thought of the Mother, I ached to return, yet I felt as if she were pushing me away. I wondered if I had done something to be rejected of the blessing she had bestowed on me months before. Thankfully, there was time to make my decision.

The role I had taken on did not prevent my further attempts at training. In fact, the time I had to train was the most useful time to subtly feel out the different Races and Clans on their positions. The Masters were all intelligent enough to know what I was doing, yet there was no way I could get each of them to open up as thoroughly with their sworn enemy in the room. One thing was clear. Once Eorpe had been returned to the Mother, and man had been eliminated as a threat to our existence, the Races would return to their previous dispositions with one another. A few centuries didn't erase a millennia of history.

A training session with Neenjta, a Dwarven Sorceress of high regard, led me to question the entirety of our return. "TaeKuz, think of the risks. You personally know the drain casting inflicts on someone in Aaru better than anyone. There are several of us who hope to muster the power to carry ourselves through with the veil weakened, but what of those who have little to no magical skill? Will you depend on us to carry the others through? Will you separate the clans and families that cannot carry themselves?"

This was most definitely a new issue to resolve. "If I were to split the families, there is no guarantee we will ever have another chance to reunite them. The veil will close with the solar eclipse. We have a large enough window to carry everyone through; we just need to find the means to do so.

"The dragons are still slumbering beneath Eorpe. Their power is immense, but would they assist us in the matter?"

Neenjta became visibly uncomfortable at the mention of the dragons. Dwarves often imposed on the dragon's homes as they expanded their cities beneath the mountains. The absence of dragons in Aaru prevented the two Races to find a way to coexist. "Their knowledge is vast, and with knowledge comes power. Their sole purpose is to record and keep the histories of the Mother. They care not who influences the history, only that they record the deeds of the inhabitants. There is no compromise when it comes to a dragon."

"What of the Crann'arsa? Would they be willing to contribute?"

"The relationship between my people and theirs was always of limited nature. Speak to one of yours for their opinion, but in my experience, they would have nothing to offer. The Crann'arsa were of little benefit unless you find it useful to bury roots and destroy beautifully carved caverns and halls. Their roots would send cracks spider-webbing through our homes, yet they claimed to be a peaceful race. No one was more glad for the fires that burned the majority of that pesky tree race to ash than I."

Neenjta's frustration was obvious. I would get no helpful advice from her. "Do you desire to return at all? Are you telling me to find a way to ruin the plans altogether?"

"How could you ask such a thing? Of course I wish to return to the Mother. I can no longer remember the aroma of damp stone being cut and shaped to house our kind. Nor do I remember the beauty of jewels and gold glittering beneath a starlit sky as we return from a raid. Do not dare to imply an atrocity such as that. I desire nothing more than to return."

"It is settled then," I said. "You will lead the first party to Eorpe. Your skill will be needed in both disguising the party and preparing the way for the final return. You will attempt peace with the dragons, as well. What better ambassador than a humble dwarf willing to set aside old feuds to establish new relations with an old 'friend'? Our return is a pivotal point in the history of Eorpe, and the time has come for them to be a part of the making instead of only recording."

With that, I turned and walked away. My training session was not complete, and I could have vanished, but I wanted her to see the authority I held in that moment. Her anger was as hot as the dragon flames awaiting her on Eorpe. "You self-centered youngling. Elves like yourself are the reason we are here to begin with."

I turned to smile and wave as I vanished to find my grandfather. Control and power invigorated me in a way I had never felt. A voice whispered caution in my ear, but I easily brushed away. Grandfather had a few questions to answer, and then I would enlighten him on the fact that he would be returning sooner rather than later.

CHAPTER SIX

*T*here was no reason to be stealthy as I stormed up to my grandfather, interrupting his conversation with a group unfamiliar to me. Faces ranged from disgust at the interruption to shock that I would dare. Perhaps it was the position of power I had been given, but at that moment, I was careless to the concerns of others, no matter how much my elder.

"Grandfather, we have urgent matters to discuss."

His ethereal face read of embarrassment and fear. "TaeKuz, what gives you the right to interrupt my comrades? We have very important matters to discuss ourselves, and like it or not, you must wait."

"Grandfather," I took a deep breath to settle my nerves and give myself an image of authority, "that is not an option."

My gaze took in the unknown individuals, or at least the ones I could see beneath their cowls. Each race was represented from what I could ascertain; the balance was missing, however. In all things from the beginning of time, there was a required balance. Call it Light and Dark, Good and Evil, or whatever you will. There was no need for a title, as each race knew where they fell. No title could explain the truth behind a race's cohesion with the Mother's will.

Evil is defined as morally wrong or bad, but no race was *truly* evil. They each simply held their one role in the Mother's wishes to keep balance. Some may have had more evil pretenses, but within even those, there were different levels between clans and tribes. Furthermore, each clan or tribe would then have members that held different roles within them. The same for the benevolent side of the balance.

The balance was astray, I realized, as I felt the hatred and disgust rolling from each individual, including my grandfather. "Sir, if you do not have time for me then I will make this short. The details can be discussed at a later time more convenient to you, but you will be returning to Eorpe with Neenjta on the first return. I will remain here to prepare the rest."

Turning my head, I slowly took in the reactions of each of the members of his group. Fury continued to build as I turned and stalked off dismissively.

A voice followed me, light but laced with rage. "How dare he imply that he has the authority to tell you to return? His place is at the front line as you 'foretold,' and you must remind him of such. The whole of our plan depends on this."

Oh yes, Grandfather. We most definitely have a few things to discuss.

CHAPTER SEVEN

"*A*igWist, you need to find a way to reel in that grandson of yours. I went out on a limb for you, vouching for you with the Faction, and you let him go and order the two of us to return. And the disgrace he brought to you by interrupting your meeting!"

"Hush. I don't want to hear your criticism, Neenjta. You were to keep him occupied with his training until we had completed the final devices of the plan. I understand that he must become a martyr to the cause, but I was attempting to at least make his death quick and painless. I'll be fortunate if they afford me that rite at this point.

"You should have seen their faces. If they thought they could change his mind without my assistance, I would not have walked away. Thankfully, they are well aware that his father would never consider their goal as a feasible one. My son does not seek the glorification of replacing me on the Council, so for now he sits quietly in the shadows waiting to guide his son to glory. For centuries I felt the same, but I have come to the realization that the only way to return to our glory is for Man to pay."

The space they shared was empty, conjured solely within a place in their minds that they chose to share. Two of the most powerful sorcerers who existed within the space of Aaru, or the history of Eorpe for that matter. They had no need to conjure images of one another or surroundings to put them at ease. To them, the comfort was within the connection they had built, one long forbidden. A devotion of love spanning the races, counterweights to the balance of the universe and the Mother.

"Yes, my love. Man will pay. We will enslave the people who forced us to leave the Mother, and torture them slowly as they have done unto her. The Faction will not accept the changes to their plan easily. You must attempt to change TaeKuz's mind, but if you are unable, we must take solace that we will return together."

"Moving him from a position that he has taken is as nearly impossible as uprooting a Crann'arsa from a favored creek bank, but I will make an attempt. Time is short. Something I never thought I would have to worry about again. Make your preparations. We must be prepared if I fail."

AigWist gave his beloved a kiss before venturing off to speak with his grandson. Unsure how he would accomplish the task set before him, he chose to compile a short list of others that he would wish to return with him. If they were to succeed, they would need the most talented that could be spared. However, if fate were against them and failure became reality, he would want to ensure that anyone with knowledge of their hidden agenda was with him. Ultimately, AigWist's goal was to keep his family safe. Despite the Faction's plan developed from his vision to make TaeKuz a martyr, and the frustrations the youngling was giving him, AigWist secretly sought a way to keep him from harm.

This would mark an unprecedented time in history, when the names of the entire Faction would be given to someone outside their circle. They would be the first to return.

AUTHOR K. LASLIE

K. LASLIE resides in Louisville, KY with an amazing wife and two sons. When not being pulled in every direction possible with the normal tasks of life, he enjoys working in the wood shop as well as breeding and raising tropical fish. He didn't find his love for reading until meeting his wife, however now it is rare to find him without a book in hand. While he had no intention to start writing until a friend challenged him to do so, he quickly found that he was hooked and couldn't wait to get his first book done and start on the second.

Admitting that there is a time an e-reader comes in handy, he still prefers to hold the real thing when reading. While in the past he only read fantasy and dystopian for the most part, after getting to know several indie authors at a local signing he attended with his wife, he is now open to giving all genres a shot.

Find out more about him and read a free excerpt of his upcoming horror novel at his website: twoauthorsonemind.wordpress.com

EXILED

JENNIFER LASLIE

CHAPTER ONE

*M*aylene had felt something off in her magic all week.

She staggered down the hall and braced herself in the doorway to her room. A surge of magical energy coursed down her legs and dropped her to her knees, forcing a startled cry from her lips. Honeyed tendrils framed her face as she stared at the floor, chest heaving.

Muffled footsteps resonated down the hall — her guards. They found their Queen on her hands and knees, trying to catch her breath.

"Your Majesty, we heard you cry out. Are you hurt?"

The guards didn't dare touch her, but they blocked off the area to protect her. Their eyes were ever alert to possible danger, searching every nook and cranny of the hallway.

"I'm fine." Maylene finally caught her breath. Bracing her hand against the doorframe, she stood up slowly. It was only a matter of time before another rush of magic poured through her. "Help me to my bed," she ordered.

Two guards broke from the ranks and positioned themselves on either side of her. Together, they guided Maylene, the Queen of the Summer Court, to her bed. The guard on her left released her arm and took great care in pulling the covers back as she eased onto the plush surface.

Lucian dashed into the room and ran quickly to her side. "Are you all right?"

"Yes, husband. I am fine." She didn't want to alarm him to her condition. He would worry something fierce, when she herself had already resolved the issue in her mind.

"No worries, dear. We'll call the healer to come look you over. Just to be safe." His hands gently smoothed down her hair and cupped her cheeks. "I won't leave anything to chance."

Maylene sighed in resignation. "Fine." She was stubborn, but she knew when to pick her battles.

Lucian turned to the nearest guard, Frederick. "Go send for Telda and tell her not to dally. The Queen needs her attention."

Frederick bowed his head and made haste out the door.

Minutes later, a wizened old woman entered Maylene's bed-chambers. Her white hair piled loosely atop her head in a semblance of a bun. Lines creased her face at every angle, bespeaking of the time she'd lived in Faerie. She was human, but she possessed magical abilities that were helpful to others in the realm.

Telda stepped up to Maylene's bedside and pressed a hand to the queen's forehead. Her tiny hand lifted and hovered over different areas of Maylene's body. Telda sensed something was off in the Queen's energies.

Delicately, Telda's fingers waved over Maylene's abdomen. A smile alighted her face. "Your Majesty. Congratulations are in order!" She pulled her hand back and, with more spirit than a woman of her age should have, she jumped and rushed over to Lucian. "Our Queen is with child. Two, in fact!"

"Twins?" His mouth hung open, but no other words came out.

"Yes!" Telda giddily leapt from foot to foot.

"B-but," Maylene stuttered, "we'd given up on ever conceiving. It's been decades and nothing."

Telda tutted. "These things take time, and fate has finally granted your heart's desire. I think news like this calls for a celebration!"

Lucian sat on the edge of his wife's bed and turned toward Telda. "Shouldn't we be concerned with the spells the Queen has been having?"

Maylene gasped. "You've noticed?"

"How could I not?" Lucian wrapped his arm around Maylene and pulled her close. "There isn't much you can hide from me."

Telda waved her hands over Maylene once again, assessing at a deeper level. "This isn't anything new, my dear. It's simply how a pregnancy goes with a faerie child — well, *children*. They can sometimes come into their powers at conception, and the mother gives off residual effects. One of your offspring seems quite powerful."

Both Lucian and Maylene smiled.

"I think that's a good thing, husband," Maylene whispered.

Telda paid them no mind as the pair continued to stare at each other. "You'll need to let me check you regularly to make sure things are progressing adequately. Perhaps once a month, until you get closer to term. If you have any more unusual magical spikes, let me know."

"I certainly will, Telda. Thank you so much for your promptness and for relieving my fears." Maylene's smile lit up the room. Pregnancy really did suit her.

Instinctively, her hand rested on her flat abdomen. Soon, it would bloom and flourish with life; life she had waited too long for. She would have a child to which she could pass on her kingdom. No… She would have *two*.

A niggling tendril of fear snaked its way through her. How would she decide who would rule? Gender made no difference in their kingdom. She had ruled alone forever before she found Lucian. Being firstborn made no difference, either. In this world, the strongest survived.

Lucian watched a myriad of emotions toy with the worry lines on her face. He squeezed her hand reassuringly, always best at reading her emotions. "All will be well, my love. Don't worry about something that has yet to happen."

CHAPTER TWO

"*L*ucian!" Maylene screamed from the kitchen. She clutched the edge of the counter as a wave of powerful magic coursed down her fingers and into the granite countertop. The current sizzled and flared towards the corners. Sparks flew and lit a nearby rag on fire.

Nadya, one of the kitchen workers, rushed in and gasped at the sight. The Queen's face was flushed red from exertion, her knuckles white from her grasp on the counter.

"M'lady?" Nadya questioned.

Lucian rushed in behind the girl and crushed Maylene to his chest. "Are you okay? Was it the babies again?"

Maylene, though breathless from this latest spell, still managed to exhale the word *yes.*

Nadya finally snapped out of her daze and rushed to put the fire out. She yanked the towel off its perch and threw it to the tiled floor, stomping on it. The smell of magic and smoke permeated the air.

"Maylene, this has to stop. I don't know if you or I can take much more. There has to be something to keep their magic from overpowering you." Lucian stepped back from his wife and paced the kitchen while Nadya made herself invisible near the cupboard.

The Queen waved him off. "I'll be fine."

"You set the kitchen on fire!" Lucian's voice was louder than he intended. He softened his next words. "We need to find a solution. Perhaps Telda can assist you."

"Not right now. This incident was strong. I usually only have one a day when it's that powerful. I don't think I'll have another occurrence soon." She rubbed her lower back, still feeling the ache from the last blast of magic. Being six months pregnant put some wear and tear on her back, as well. "I'll speak with her tonight. I need to get a breath of fresh air. Would you like to take a walk with me, my love?" Maylene crooked her arm and held it out.

Lucian let out an exasperated sigh, but conceded. He took Maylene by her arm, even though he'd rather pull out his golden hair at the roots. She was the love of his life. He would take care of her the best way he could, but he couldn't force her to do anything she didn't want to. She was stubborn like that.

Her stubbornness was what attracted him to her in the first place. She was always headstrong and willful. She had to be when running the Summer Court.

They stepped out into the tepid morning air, arm-in-arm. Maylene pulled him toward the well-worn path in the tree line that led down to the lake.

Out of breath, she reclined on a wooden bench near the edge of the water. Small waves lapped against the bank. The atmosphere was peaceful for both of them.

"Do you think we'll be good parents?" Maylene probed. She still worried about raising two children and having to decide who would rule.

"You're going to be a wonderful mother. You have nothing to worry about." Lucian brought his hand over to rest on her distended abdomen. The two babies within wriggled at his touch.

"Now, isn't this a sweet little moment?" A slender figure stepped around the bend in the lake, emerging from the trees. Her soft blue hair glistened in the morning light as if made of ice. Cold, cerulean eyes pierced the couple with a stare.

Lucian stood up from the bench and blocked Lorinda's path to his wife. "What are you doing here? Shouldn't you be in a colder climate?" His hand lingered at his side near his dagger. Despite his calm demeanor, he would end that wicked woman's reign in a heartbeat.

Lorinda leaned ever so slightly to see around Lucian. "Why, I heard the good news and came to offer my congratulations. Word has spread that you are blessed with not one, but two!" Her eyes lit up with fascination. Probably the warmest they'd been in ages. The babies intrigued her.

Conceiving at all was hard enough, but to find yourself expecting two? That was a miracle. The Winter Queen went to great lengths to get pregnant with her son. It had taken decades for her to conceive a child, as well as many suitors. He was probably toddling about the palace at this very moment, still so very young.

"You have delivered your message as courtesy dictates. Your congratulations have been received." Maylene stood up and moved to stand beside Lucian. "But I think you've overstayed your welcome."

"Maylene. I'm crushed!" Lorinda feigned injury, clutching her chest. "You wound me." She didn't keep up the act for long. Her hand was by her side once again before Maylene or Lucian could blink.

"You're no more hurt than I am blind. What is your real reason for this visit?" Lucian couldn't take anymore from this vile beast of a queen. She didn't deserve the title. Her voice grated on his nerves, and her presence made him sick.

Lorinda stared off into nothing for a moment. Was she daydreaming? That seemed absurd considering the circumstances. Finally, she waved her hand absently in the air. "Fine, fine, fine. I'll take my leave. I can see when I'm not wanted."

Lorinda's slim form drifted away through the trees and out of sight.

Maylene released the breath she was holding and cradled her abdomen. "That woman… She drives me mad!"

Lucian pulled his wife into his arms and comforted her. "Pay her no mind. It was only her sick curiosity that brought her here. She can't harm our children. Once they are born, I'll have 'round the clock guards watching over the two." His hand gently rubbed circles on her back.

"She already has a child. I don't know why ours should even be any concern to her." Maylene huffed as she backed out of Lucian's arms. "I've had enough fresh air. Let's go see what Telda can do about these episodes."

CHAPTER THREE

*L*orinda sat idly on her throne, twirling a ceramic cup by its handle. "Those little brats are powerful. I could feel the magical energy radiating from her."

Emery sat in the middle of the throne room with his wooden blocks. He'd stacked them up quite high. There were at least fifteen piled on top of each other, wobbling slightly. His small two-year-old frame stood nimbly beside his tower. Emery was very smart for his age and excelled at almost everything he did.

Tiny hands grasped the sixteenth block. Transferring the toy block to his left hand, he held out his right hand, willing the blocks to align under each other. The tower didn't wobble anymore. With a grin of satisfaction on his face, he placed the next block.

"You've always been so bright, Emery. I need to find a way to bind you to one of the children she's having." Her free hand smoothed over her dress. "Yes, that'll do nicely. Or better yet, if I siphoned one of their powers... Oh, the possibilities are endless!" She twirled the cup a moment longer before dropping it unceremoniously onto the marble floor, the clatter shattering the silence and the cup.

"Come, Emery. We have plans to make." She scooped up the toddler and whisked him out of the room, his tower forgotten. If she was going to succeed, she needed to figure out the best strategy.

§

TELDA ENTERED THE BEDCHAMBER to find Maylene tucked into bed, her husband by her side. Brynna, Telda's assistant, came into the room behind her. Together, they checked the queen over and observed she was in perfect health.

"The only issue you have is the power from the babes. There is naught I can do for you while you still carry them but advise you to rest and wait until delive — "

Suddenly, Telda's eyes transformed into murky white orbs. Her hand grasped Maylene's leg tightly. Her voice dipped into a low, raspy monotone, the voice that always took over when a vision or prediction forced itself upon her unexpectedly.

> *A child of Peace and a child of Strife,*
> *Two girls shall you soon give life.*
> *One will destroy Faerie in towers of fire,*
> *One will give the joy you so desire.*
> *Grown together, torn apart,*
> *Youth reveals the seeds of heart.*
> *No good comes from both alive;*
> *A single child must survive,*
> *Or all of Faerie will surely die.*

As suddenly as Telda's eyes had clouded over, they turned back to their dark brown state. She collapsed to the ground in a heap of weariness. Having visions always taxed her.

Maylene gasped and curled in on herself. The beautiful queen, who was always regal and imposing, now brought down to size from the words the old woman had uttered.

"Telda? I'm-I'm going to have to kill one of my children? That's not possible! They're not even born yet!" The queen raged against the outcome she knew must happen. How could she put her realm in jeopardy? She'd have to end a precious life. Children were already a rarity in Faerie. She wasn't sure if she could bring herself to do it.

Brynna was immediately by Telda's side, propping her up to check for injuries.

Telda's voice was but a whisper. "You must do what is good for Faerie."

Lucian had been speechless until this point. "Guards, please help Telda to her room where she may rest. She's had quite an ordeal this evening." He gestured towards Frederick and Bronin as he stepped around Telda. He sat down on the edge of the bed and pulled Maylene into his arms. They both had a hard decision to make in the coming months. Should they be selfish? Telda had been inaccurate before, and free will could not be eliminated through predictions. A faerie always had a chance to change their fate.

"What are we going to do, Lucian?" Fat tears rolled down Maylene's cheeks, hovered on her chin, then dropped below to soak into the blanket. Her shoulders shook as she leaned forward to muffle her sobs in Lucian's shirt.

The others in the room left to give the Summer King and Queen their space to mourn their decisions, whether right or wrong. Neither knew what lay ahead of them with either choice. If both children received love and care, why would either one of them want to harm their family or home?

The difficult decision lodged tightly in Maylene's throat. There was no easy answer.

CHAPTER FOUR

ime sped up beyond reason for both the king and queen, once they had come to the decision that only one of the children should survive. The only other difficult decision would be picking which daughter should live and which daughter should perish.

Telda had been right on another account: A celebration was in order, despite the occasional knee-buckling surge of magic that racked Maylene's body.

Tonight, the whole of Faerie would turn out to help the Summer Court celebrate the upcoming delivery of the new heirs. It was too late to try to keep the twins' arrival a secret. Word had spread far and wide that there would be two children born to the Summer Queen.

Maylene's only concern was the devastation that would ensue once word spread about the death of one. It would cause a rippling effect of grief and sorrow. There would still be life, however. One child would survive to rule over the Summer Court.

Exquisite smells permeated the air as Maylene waddled through the halls toward the kitchen.

"My Queen!" One of the kitchen staff dropped to a knee as Maylene entered.

"Up with you! I won't get any food in my belly with all of you kneeling or bowing." Maylene ran a hand over her rotund abdomen, as she smelled the air. Hints of breads, sweets, and roasted meat hung heavy, and Maylene's mouth watered.

"Of course! I will get you a plate straightaway!" The petite woman jumped to her feet and began busily making a plate. She piled it with slices of meats, cubes of different cheeses, soft buttered biscuits, and a myriad of other delicacies.

The kitchen staff would be working nonstop to get everything prepared in time for the huge feast this evening. Maylene always boasted of her kitchen staff's culinary skills.

Once the plate was full to the brim, the petite woman stood before Maylene. "Would you like me to bring this to the table for you, My Queen?"

"Oh! Yes, that would be most helpful." Maylene turned to follow the spry woman toward the dining hall.

The servant lay the plate at one of the many place settings, and Maylene sank into the cushioned chair with a contented sigh.

The woman bowed deeply and then raced back towards the kitchen. Maylene had her fork poised over her plate when a guard ran in.

"My Queen!" He came to an abrupt halt beside her chair.

"Is the palace on fire, Bronin?" Maylene lifted a brow.

"No, your Majesty. The king asked me to come get you. He wants to make sure that the decorations are to your liking before we open the doors tonight." Bronin stood stoically.

"The *king* can wait until I've fed his children and myself." Maylene chuckled as she resumed her eating.

Bronin dropped his rigid stance and waited patiently. He knew from experience that it wouldn't take the queen that long to eat. She'd wipe that plate clean within seconds.

§

MAYLENE STOOD IN THE spacious ballroom and slowly spun in a circle, taking in all of the beautiful pink decorations adorning the room. There were wide pink ribbons hung across each wall. Soft rose-colored tablecloths draped over the tables where the guests could enjoy the feast. The napkins, placeholder cards, and even the centerpieces were pink.

The only thing not decorated in pink was the massively long table in the back, which would hold all the food.

Pink was the obvious choice, of course, since they were expecting twin girls.

Perfect. It was perfect.

"Do you approve, dear?" Lucian's eyes shown with such love and adoration. He would stop at nothing to see her smile. He lived to make her happy. When she was happy, he was happy.

"Yes," she breathed. "I love it. All of it!" Her laughter carried through the massive room.

"I'm glad." Lucian swept her up into a side hug, spinning her around.

"Woah, now! Not too much of that. You'll make me sick."

Lucian planted Maylene's feet back on the ground as she clutched him tightly.

"Are you okay?" He hadn't meant to startle her or make her sick.

"Yes." Her hands instinctively circled over her extended belly. She was already seven months pregnant. She knew with carrying twins that she wouldn't make it to nine months.

She honestly hadn't expected to make it this long. How much more could her belly take? Her breath hitched, and she let out a groan.

"Maylene?" Lucian's arms supported her.

"I told you. I'm fine. One of the girls just kicked too hard, is all. You worry too much." She brushed him off. "I need to go get ready for the celebration."

§

SEATED UPON THE DAIS, the Summer King and Queen watched as each guest was announced. In turn, the guests approached and congratulated the expecting couple, then placed their gift on the ever-growing pile.

Maylene observed guests from her own kingdom as well as from the Fall, Winter, and Spring courts. The land of the Fae was divided into the four seasons. Each respective season helped both Faerie and the human world to thrive. Without them, life could not exist. Balance was paramount. Yet, it was becoming increasingly difficult for the Fae to reproduce.

The population in all the courts was slowly dwindling. The human world was oblivious; most humans no longer believed in fairy tales or the Fae. That was the problem; their belief was one of the many things that helped keep Faerie alive.

The ballroom had filled up quite nicely. People milled about, talking and dancing to the small quartet of violins that played beautifully in the corner.

The herald proclaimed, "Announcing... Queen Lorinda Cantwell of the Winter Court!"

A hush fell over the crowd. No one had truly expected the Winter Queen to make an appearance. The Summer Queen and Winter Queen had never gotten along. It wasn't the fault of the Summer Queen. She had tried her best to make amends to whatever offense she may have given.

Regally, the Winter Queen proceeded down the stairs into the ballroom, her head held high, nose in the air, as if she were better than everyone within the vicinity. She believed she was, too.

Lorinda's soft blue hair lay in waves down her back. A silver crown inlaid with ice blue diamonds adorned her head, twinkling in the candlelight from the chandeliers.

The Winter Queen stepped up to the dais and smoothed both hands down her pristine white gown. She held no gift.

No one said a word. The crowd held their breath, waiting for the altercation to unfold.

Lorinda bowed to no one. She inclined her head toward Maylene and Lucian.

"Good evening." Lorinda's hands folded in front of her, knuckles white with restraint. She could still feel the power emanating from Maylene. Those babes had more power in their little fingers than she did in her whole body, and she wanted it, craved it. "I've come to offer my congratulations on the brat...err, babies. It is rare indeed to be blessed with twins."

Maylene could see Lorinda's struggle to be cordial, but she returned the courtesy in kind, forgiving Lorinda the slip of the tongue. "Lorinda, so lovely of you to come."

Lucian interjected, trying to divert Lorinda's attention away from his wife. "Thank you, Lorinda, Queen of the Winter Court. We have no qualms here. Today is a celebration of life. Stay, eat, drink, and enjoy yourself."

Lorinda inclined her head once again in acknowledgement and disappeared into the crowd.

Once the Winter Queen was away from the dais, the crowd's murmurs strengthened. Speculations built, fresh rumors started, and wayward glances were thrown in the Winter Queen's direction.

Lorinda heard their whispers and ignored them. *Let them talk.* Most of what they said was probably true. Some of the winter town folk gathered around her. Together, they were stronger. Their magic helped fuel hers.

The only problem was that the winter court was dwindling faster than any other court. Lorinda planned to change that.

CHAPTER FIVE

*T*he celebration concluded. No trouble occurred, and many of the partygoers ate and drank their fill, then retired for the night. Maylene's heart had skipped a beat when Lorinda had arrived. She would have been no match for the Winter Queen in her condition. She could barely move, let alone walk.

Having slipped away early on in the celebration, due to exhaustion, Maylene slept soundly in her bedchamber.

Much later than expected, the King had sidled up next to her to retire for the evening, as well.

It was just after three in the morning when Maylene awoke, a lightning bolt of pain shooting through her abdomen. Her cries rang through the palace.

Lucian all but fell out of bed, having woken from a dead sleep. He'd had a few glasses of wine last night and wasn't in the best shape to deal with the onslaught of noise.

"Maylene?" he mumbled groggily.

"The babies!" She sat up, hunching over her belly, and groaned. "Oh my goodness! I think they're coming!"

"What?" Lucian's jaw dropped. "Now?!" He shuffled towards the dresser, then back to the bed, at a loss for what he needed to do. "But it's not time yet!"

"It doesn't matter." Maylene pushed the covers aside and slid out of bed. "We have to find Telda and Brynna." She wrapped her arms around her abdomen, crying out again as magic zinged down her legs, out of her bare feet, and sizzled on the stone floor.

Lucian ran around the bed and supported Maylene, but small

sparks of magic arced between them, and he backed away quickly. "Stay here. I'll go get them and be right back."

"No! Don't leave me!" Maylene still had one arm clutched to her belly as the other reached out to him.

"I...I can't do anything for you without them." He threw the door open and looked both ways down the hall. "Guards!"

His shout rang down the corridor. A couple guards had the night watch; surely, one of them would hear the commotion.

"Lucian!" Maylene reached the doorway just as her water broke, making the stone floor slick. "Go! The guards can't hear you. Find Telda and hurry back."

Lucian didn't wait another second as he raced down the hall toward Telda's room. He had to wake the healer and get her back to his wife before it was too late.

Bursting through the door, Lucian went straight to Telda's bed and found it empty. Panicking, he ran back out into the hallway and began searching for a guard.

He found Bronin, one of his most loyal men, standing near the main entrance to the palace. "Oh, Bronin." Lucian tried to catch his breath. "I'm so glad I found you."

"What is it, Your Majesty?" Concern etched Bronin's face.

"The Queen. The babies." His hands gestured wildly. "They're coming! Have you seen Telda?" Lucian was beside himself. He'd left Maylene all alone while she was in labor.

Bronin raised a hand and pointed. "Sire, I saw her heading towards the kitchen about thirty minutes ago."

"Thank you! Please fetch Telda and bring her to my chambers. I need to get back to the queen." Lucian pushed the guard towards the kitchen as he ran in the other direction back to his wife.

Relief washed over him as he found her back in bed and not lying on the floor. He approached with caution and held out a tentative hand as he smoothed down her hair. "How are you feeling?" He was thankful he wasn't greeted with the electrical shock of magic.

"I feel horrible. The contractions are close, and I cannot control the magic from them when they get distressed." Sweat coated Maylene's face, making her hair stick to her sallow skin. Her breathing was heavy.

"For crying out loud, I go to make me a sandwich and can't even take the first bite of it without getting interrupted by this imbecile," Telda muttered as she stepped over to Maylene. "Now, what's all the fuss about?"

Bronin stood in the doorway at a loss for words. Telda could be rather feisty in her old age. He shrugged when Lucian glanced his way.

"Telda, the queen has gone into labor. The babies are coming." Lucian wrung his hands together.

"Well, I can see that now." She waved a hand in the air. "Bronin, go see if Brynna is awake. I'll need her assistance. She'll know what to bring."

Bronin didn't need to be told twice. He didn't want to be anywhere near that room when the queen gave birth.

"Let's check you over and see how much longer you have." Telda shuffled up next to Maylene, scooting Lucian out of the way. Her nimble fingers palpated Maylene's abdomen. "They've dropped, all right."

Another anguished scream erupted from Maylene as the contraction hit. If this was how every labor was, it was a good thing she was having two. Then, the realization hit her. She wasn't having two. One was to be sentenced to death for merely existing.

Her cries of pain turned into hiccupping sobs, and she couldn't stop the tears from flowing.

"Are you in that much pain, dearie?" Telda inquired. "I can make you a draught to help take the edge off."

"No, no. I was just thinking about… Well, what needs to be done once I've given birth to the two of them." Maylene choked on her sobs, trying to compose herself before continuing. "How will I choose?"

Telda's face softened. This choice would affect the whole kingdom, and thus it was not something to be taken lightly. "When the time comes, you'll know. Perhaps we should take the strongest and healthiest of the two so they have the best chance at survival?"

"That… Yes, that's what we'll do." Maylene nodded in agreement.

Lucian remained quiet, standing vigil by the door, waiting for Brynna.

"My King, let's strip the bed down and get the queen comfortable. We'll need a couple more pillows to help prop her up." Telda pulled the comforter off the bed, and then turned to Lucian. "Do you think you could get those pillows, please?"

Snapping out of his daze, Lucian gave a nod and left the room.

"We'll keep him busy so he doesn't feel helpless." Telda chuckled. She helped move Maylene to a more comfortable position, and Lucian came back with pillows just in time.

Brynna finally arrived, with Bronin in tow, carrying all of the supplies they would need.

For the next four hours, the Queen labored. Her normally honey-colored hair lacked luster, matted to her head with sweat. She couldn't quite catch her breath between contractions, and the magical surges were putting Telda at a disadvantage.

By some miracle, the first child finally arrived into the world, a startled cry spilling out into the room as Brynna cleaned her up. She had a full head of blonde hair and sparkling blue eyes.

Brynna smiled down at the first child. "What are you going to name her?" It hadn't been determined which child would live. It was dependent on how healthy the second child was. In Faerie, only the strongest survived.

"I've chosen Alandra and Helena."

The second baby took another twenty minutes to come into the world. She was an exact copy of her sister, but was the larger of the two. She looked healthier and livelier. Her lungs were rather healthy, as well.

"Let me see them," begged the Queen.

Brynna brought the second, healthier child over to Maylene and placed her in the Queen's outstretched arms.

"She's gorgeous," cooed Maylene. "Just beautiful. Which child is this?"

"It is your only child," stated Telda plainly. "Do you not remember? Only one child survived. This child shall be your heir, Helena."

"What do you mean only one child survived? I heard two cries!" The queen was frantic. She repositioned herself, sitting up and searching the room.

Brynna had already slipped out with the first child, the smaller of the two.

"My Queen, you knew only one could live. The fate of Faerie hung in the balance. The healthier child will live," Telda explained with a note of melancholy.

"Telda, I've changed my mind! I don't want one of them to die." The child in her arms started to cry, sensing her mother's distress. "You have to bring her back to me! That's my child!"

"It's already done. What is done cannot be undone," Telda intoned.

The queen screamed in rage, causing the baby in her arms to cry even louder.

"You must calm down." Telda placed a soothing hand on the Queen's arm. "You're scaring your child. She needs you now, more than ever. You should feed her."

"I can't!" Maylene stifled out between sobs. "What have I done?"

"You've done what's best for your kingdom." Telda tried to remain strong, but her resolve was slipping. She mourned the loss of the child just as much as her queen.

§

BRYNNA HAD SWADDLED THE first child tightly in a blanket and slipped out into the hall per Telda's instructions. She was to take her far from the palace and dispose of her in the woods.

At first, the child remained calm in her arms, her eyes closed, soft lashes feathered against her cheeks. The further Brynna trudged into the woods, the more the child seemed aware of her fate. She started to whimper. Soon, those whimpers turned into cries, and then morphed into wails of despair.

The baby's panic ignited magical surges. Brynna had prepared for them. She'd used her own magical abilities to erect a shield around her for just this situation. It wasn't fool proof, however. Small amounts of the infant's magic still breached Brynna's magical shield.

Brynna halted her progress, leaning against a massive tree to ground herself. She cradled the child in her arms and lifted the blanket covering her face.

Her blues eyes pierced Brynna to the core.

Brynna gasped, realizing she couldn't kill this child. She was a child of Faerie, which was something too precious to waste. She did the only other thing she could think of to save the child's life, and yet still save Faerie: She bound the girl's powers, locking them away deep within the recesses of her mind. No one would be able to find her magical signature.

Locating the entrance to the human world, Brynna stepped through it, her ears popping. There was a distinct difference in the atmosphere within the human realm. The humans didn't care how they treated the planet.

Immediately, Brynna put up her glamour to hide her otherworldly features. Walking swiftly, she took the infant to a nearby a fire station. The humans had a law about unwanted offspring. She'd receive the care she needed and a home where she would be safe.

Brynna hesitated at the fire station's door. Raising a hand, she finally pushed the buzzer. The door clicked, and she pushed it open with her shoulder.

A young man in a Worthington Fire Department t-shirt stepped up to her. "How can I help you, ma'am?"

"I was told that any child could be dropped off here. I…I found this baby abandoned in the woods." Brynna lifted up the blanket from the baby's face, showing just how new the child was to this world. "This is a safe place, right?"

The man wore a troubled expression, but knew that he had no right to ask any questions. The fire station was indeed a safe place. He merely nodded and reached for the child. "Would you mind filling out a form? You can provide whatever information you might have."

"Could I name her? She needs someone to give her a name, right?" Before she'd slipped from the queen's bedchamber, Brynna had heard Telda name the other child Helena. She would give this child the second name the queen had picked out.

"That shouldn't be a problem. Follow me." He gestured with his head and led her into an office. "I'm Lieutenant Ashby. You don't have to give me your name."

Brynna nodded as he sat down in his chair.

He held the baby in one arm as his other hand pulled open a drawer in his desk. His fingers deftly flipped through some folders until he pulled out two pieces of paper stapled together and laid them before Brynna.

"Fill these out as best you can, and I'll be right back." He stood, taking the child with him.

Brynna couldn't fill out most of the information, but for the child's name, she wrote *Alandra*. She put a few other pieces of information she thought would be helpful and slipped out before the lieutenant could return.

She had to get back to Faerie before her absence was noted.

AUTHOR JENNIFER LASLIE

JENNIFER LASLIE lives in Louisville, KY with her wonderful husband, 2 kids, 4 dogs, 3 cats and mother-in-law. She has always been an avid reader. She loves Young Adult, Dystopian, and Paranormal Romance.

Find her online at authorjlaslie.weebly.com.

If you enjoyed *EXILED*,
check out *PERSUADING TOMORROW*

When the unimaginable happens and Jordan loses her best friend on the night she had planned to tell him her feelings, it leaves her to wonder if she's the guilty party, but her memories of that night are fuzzy. In an attempt to leave her past and the hateful stares of her peers behind, she moves across the country to live with her mother in Esterwilde, Pennsylvania. It's a small close-knit town, but there no one should know about her past, or so she thought.

When Zyler runs into the new girl in town he can't help but feel a connection, but he also knows her past harbors a horrible secret. He's heard the rumors, but doesn't believe them. Seeing Jordan in pain kills him and all he wants to do is take it away.

Jordan soon realizes that no matter what she does she's not going to be able to outrun her past. Can Zyler show her that despite the hate and ignorance in the world that life is still worth living? Will she ever figure out the truth about the night that took away her best friend?

Available at Amazon.

§

CyberWitch Press experienced a significant backlog over the summer of 2016, and as a result, rescheduled the *Broomsticks* anthology (originally due for release in October).

But one flirty, hilarious entry *needed* to be read, especially after so many heavy fairy stories! I pride my anthologies on breaking genre barriers, mixing horror with the paranormal and a sprinkle of thriller and romance. Entertainment cannot be manufactured, categorized, fit into a neat little box; it's organic.

So page forward and enjoy a bonus short story: Ava Wood's lighthearted, erotic romance, *Burning Love.*

BURNING LOVE

AVA LYNN WOOD

Disclaimer:
Ava asks that you please refrain from setting fire to any establishment as this is a work of fiction.

CHAPTER ONE

"What time is he supposed to be there?" Marilyn's platinum hair hung in front of her eyes as she asked. Most likely, she was busy setting up another display in her shop. It didn't really matter, because I'd been applying makeup to my sea-green eyes during most of the call.

Checking the time on my phone, I felt my nerves spike when I realized Kevin would be arriving in just over an hour. "He's supposed to be here at seven," I answered, trying to tamp down my nervous anxiety.

"I'm so excited for you." She smiled, finally acknowledging my image on her screen.

"God, I'm not even sure I set the spell up right." Marilyn had given me a list of ingredients and instructions to create a concoction that was sure to make my landlord, Kevin, fall in love with me.

"Let me see," she commanded.

I walked over to the table in the living room where I'd prepared the spell. When I neared, I flipped the camera, giving her a view of the platter holding the dried rose petals, parchment paper, and red votive candle.

"What the hell is that?" she asked dubiously, her sterling eyes widening.

"What?" I *knew* I'd done something wrong.

"That's a votive candle, Elena."

"Yeah, so?" A candle was a candle, wasn't it?

"So?" She smacked her head, suddenly marching through her shop. "You need to get here, pronto."

"Is it really that big of a deal?" I knew I had no clue what I was doing, but certainly a votive candle didn't make that big of a difference.

"Yes. It is most definitely that big of a deal." I heard a jingling in the background before Marilyn said, "Get here, fast," and ended the call.

Flustered, I raced to my room, pulling the curlers out of my raven hair, then slipped on the flowery sundress that left very little to the imagination. I stepped into a pair of gold strappy sandals by the front door of my apartment before I rushed out of the house. In record time, I pulled away from the curb, running my hand through my bouncing curls, trying to style my hair as I drove.

Marilyn's shop was across town, a good fifteen minute drive, so I was going to have to keep the conversation short when I arrived. As I blew through traffic, my newly manicured nails tapped on the steering wheel, anxious to get to Marilyn's shop and back home again. I'd just remembered my quiche in the oven when I pulled into her lot.

Barging into her shop, I panted, "I'm here."

An elderly couple, looking completely out of place, stared at me as I caught my breath.

Raising a hand, I said, "I'm fine. I'm fine." Not that I assumed they cared. Shaking their heads, they turned back to look at Marilyn who was hurriedly ringing them up.

As I took a deep breath, the woodsy incense of the room worked through me, calming me instantly. I'd just started to troll through the various spell books on the shelves when I heard the door jingle and turned to watch the elderly couple walk out.

When I rounded the shelf to head toward the counter, Marilyn was smiling brightly, silently laughing as I approached.

"I hope you're not laughing at me."

She shook her head. "That was the ... craziest sale ever." Her gray eyes dipped closed as she forced her peach-tinted lips together, trying to stifle her grin.

"Okay," I muttered, waiting for some sort of explanation.

"They came in looking for oils to *spice up* their love life."

One eyebrow raised. "Are you kidding?" I fell onto a stool next to the counter, feeling quite defeated by the dry spell I'd been having. It had been damn near a year since I'd actually gotten laid. "Even the aged are getting more ass than me."

"That's going to change tonight." Marilyn winked at me before placing a small red taper candle on the counter. "Use this, but don't blow it out. Let it burn out on its own."

"Really?" I had no idea what I was doing. After our last girls' day, I'd let Marilyn convince me this was what needed to be done to get me onto Kevin's radar and out of my sexual lull. Getting into his heart would be great, but getting into his bed would be even better. At this point, I was certain that I was in way over my head.

"Trust me."

"I can't believe I let you talk me into this," I muttered, still completely clueless as to what I was really doing.

Marilyn busied herself with the till, glancing at me from the corner of her twinkling eye every now and again. "I can't believe that old couple is having more sex than you."

Scoffing, I retorted, "Not helping, Mar."

Marilyn laughed, looking me up and down. "Seriously, how does a girl with curves like you have such a problem getting lucky?"

I'd been asking myself the same question for months. "I guess I'm just not giving the right signals."

"Well, I don't think you have to worry about that tonight. That dress is sending all the right signals." Her eyebrows waggled as she grabbed the taper from the counter. "Here," She demanded, pressing it into my hand. "Take this candle and multiply." She laughed, helping me from my stool and shoving me toward the exit.

"This better work," I muttered as I fell out of the shop.

"It will. Now go." Marilyn blew me a kiss just before shutting the door and flipping the lock. With a wave of her fingers, she disappeared deep inside her store.

Jumping back in my car, I hurried home, anxious to get this whole love potion started. I didn't want Kevin walking in on me as I put the finishing touches on the parchment and lit the candle. Even though I'd tried to set it up like a *normal* centerpiece, the whole platter looked a little suspicious, at least to me.

I was just pulling into my subdivision when I noticed smoke in the distance. "What the hell?" I asked no one. I drove on, noticing that the closer I got to my home, the closer the fire appeared.

When I reached my cul-de-sac, I saw a pair of fire trucks sitting in front of Kevin's lot, actively working to put out a fire in my garage apartment.

"Oh God," I groaned, sinking into my seat once I'd pulled the car to the curb. My first thought was my poor, neglected libido, but then I remembered my helpless cat Felix who was probably stuck inside, burning to a crisp. In a complete panic, I jumped from my car, and raced for my apartment.

"Felix."

CHAPTER TWO

*F*elix!" I cried as I raced forward. When a rather robust fireman stepped forward, blocking my path, I screamed, "My poor Felix is inside," hysterically pointing at my apartment.

"Felix? He's in there?" He pointed toward the flames slithering out my kitchen window and licking the side of the building where they met the spray of water being blasted at my apartment.

"Yes, please. You have to help him."

"Men," the fireman began. Two men fully clad in their fire suits stepped forward, slipping masks over their heads.

"On it, chief," one of them said just before his voice was cut off by the mask.

In a flash, the firemen raced up the stairs and disappeared inside with axes in tow. They were out of sight for several minutes before I heard something garbled on the radio, and then the two men emerged, one with my sweet, but slightly seared Felix in his arms.

Shoving past the fire chief, I yelled, "Felix!" I barreled forward, snatching him from the fireman's arms. "My poor baby. Are you okay?"

Felix gave a very weak and scratchy meow as I rubbed his singed gray head.

"Oh my Felix. I'm so sorry." I carried him to the curb and fell to the ground, nuzzling his smoke-scented body. The smell of his head now matched the color of his fur. "So, so sorry," I repeated as I noticed large fire boots in my peripheral.

"Is he okay?" the fireman asked as he knelt down beside me, pulling the mask from his head.

Looking up, I saw the most entrancing golden eyes staring at me.

My mouth immediately went dry as I grew mesmerized by the gorgeous fireman now kneeling before me. His hair was drenched in sweat and sticking up in crazy, lascivious angles. All I could think was, *My god, he must look amazing after a romp in the sack.* I was completely unable to form a single coherent thought as I noticed the dusting of smoke on his face that gave him the sexiest, rugged allure. I really needed to get laid.

"Miss," he asked, easing closer. "Is he okay?" His glove-encased hand reached for my face, gently caressing my cheek.

Words started to form in my head, but all thought escaped me as I asked, "Is who okay?"

The fireman smiled, revealing a perfect row of sparkling teeth with canines peeking out at me, begging me to run my tongue along their sharp tips. With his lips plumped around those pearly whites, I felt my vagina cry out in agony, pleading with me for some sort of reprieve.

"Your cat," he responded around that blinding smile. "Felix, is that his name?"

"Huh? Oh. Yes. Felix." Instinctively, I scratched the top of his head, feeling those bristly burnt hairs. "I think he's okay," I finally answered.

"Oh my god. The apartment. Where's Elena?"

I heard the voice say my name from behind me and hesitantly pulled my gaze from the fireman to see Kevin racing through the chaos. As I stood, recognition crossed his face and he rushed toward me. Giving a weak smile, I called, "I'm here," then turned back toward the fireman who'd now vanished among his crew.

"What's going on? What happened?" Kevin surveyed the hose team that had just put out the fire.

"I don't know. I have no idea what happened."

Kevin reached toward me and my heart rate jumped up a notch until his hand fell to my mangy-looking cat and began scratching his side. "Were you inside?" he asked, still not completely acknowledging me.

"No," I shook my head. "I was ... I just got home from my friend's shop." I stared at him intently, waiting for him to spare me a glance.

He finally looked my way, asking, "What the hell happened to your face?"

"I ... I," I stammered, unsure of what he was referencing. I had just a touch of makeup on, but I'd tried to keep it looking natural.

When his hand fell upon my cheek, I coyly leaned into his touch. He eyed me curiously as his thumb brushed at my cheek. "What is that?" he questioned, rubbing forcefully at my cheek. "Is it dirt?"

I grimaced at the harshness of his touch, placing my hand over his to stop the offending movement.

Startlingly, he yanked his hand from mine and turned his attention to something happening over my shoulder.

"Do either of you know who the owner of this property is?" the man who'd been referenced as *Chief* asked.

"I'm the owner," Kevin answered, stepping around me. "Can you tell me what happened?"

"Looks like it was an electrical fire, sir." The chief turned toward the apartment, continuing to speak to Kevin, but all I could focus on was searching for that fireman with the dazzling smile and sparkling gold eyes.

After scanning the crew, I caught a glimpse of him, now sans coat, pouring a bottle of water over his head. I followed the trail of water as it poured over his hair and down his broad chest. The fabric of his t-shirt clung to his skin, giving way to the muscle mass beneath. Again, my mouth went dry watching him run his hand over his hair as if in slow motion.

"Elena?" Kevin called.

I pulled my attention away from that impeccable body. "Yes?"

The chief was walking away as Kevin returned to my side. "The apartment isn't a complete loss, but you can't stay there for a while. We'll have to bring the insurance company in and probably have the kitchen and living room gutted. The process could take months." His russet eyes seemed tired. Or disappointed.

I spared a quick glance to the charred windows before turning back to Kevin. "Oh," was the only response I could muster.

"Do you have a place you can stay tonight? I mean..." He pulled his lip between his teeth then stammered, "If you need a place to stay ... I guess ... I mean ... I've got that spare room."

"You're offering your spare room to me?" I should've been over the moon. This was the kind of opportunity I'd been waiting on for months, but my mind was continually drawn to that sexy-as-sin fireman.

"Well, the faulty wiring was essentially my responsibility, so I feel obligated to give you a place to stay."

Well that was good news. At least my quiche hadn't caused this fiasco. And with my entire family a half a continent away and Marilyn living with her OCD boyfriend, I didn't really have anyone else to stay with. "I'd really appreciate it. It'll help me save some money to replace everything I lost."

Kevin scratched his hand through his sandy brown hair and said, "Yeah, I guess I could help with that, too."

Was becoming a damsel in distress really the way to Kevin's heart? Now that I had his attention, all I wanted was to climb that fireman like Mount Everest, dying to reach my peak. Unfortunately, I didn't have the guts to even approach the fireman simply to ask his name.

"Elena? Are you okay?" Kevin snapped his fingers in my face, trying to get my attention.

Retrieving my tongue that was, no doubt, waggling outside my mouth, I answered, "Uh, yeah. I'm fine."

"So, will you let me put you up and help you recoup some of the stuff you lost?"

"Sure, Kevin. Thanks."

Kevin stood next to me a moment longer as I focused on the crew now loading up the truck. It wasn't until they'd long since pulled away that I headed for Kevin's house.

CHAPTER THREE

"So, how did it go last night?"

My eyes struggled to open as I listened to Marilyn cooing in my ear. Groaning, I answered, "Don't ask."

"What do you mean? The spell didn't work?" I heard pages shuffling on Marilyn's end of the line, then, "It had to work. It's always worked."

Rubbing my eyes, I admitted, "I never got the chance to try it," and groaned again. Felix jumped on the bed, curled up next to my ear, and began purring incessantly.

"What do you mean?" The skepticism in her tone was evident.

I swatted at Felix, trying to move him away from my head, but he started pawing at my hand. "Can I call you later?" I did *not* want to talk about it. Not now. Not while Felix was gnawing on my hand and purring like a lunatic. And definitely not after I tossed and turned all night dreaming about a sexy firefighter peeling his clothes off in front of me, taking me in positions only seen in the *Kama Sutra*, bringing me to orgasm in my sleep. My legs quivered remembering the way he moved next to me, above me, inside me.

"What happened?" Marilyn bemoaned. For a second, I thought I heard her massaging her temples.

On a sigh, I answered, "When I came home, the apartment was on fire."

Felix clawed my hand, inciting a slight wince and in defense, I launched him off the bed.

"What?" she screeched. "You're kidding, right?"

"I wish."

"On fire, *fire*?"

Clearly her concern for my well-being trumped my exhaustion. "Yes," I grumbled. "On fire, fire. The apartment is off limits with all of my belongings trapped inside."

"Wait, wait, wait. Off limits? So where did you sleep last night?" She didn't miss a beat.

Rubbing my forehead, I muttered, "At Kevin's."

"Oh. My. Gawd." Her voice rose an octave with each word. "Why didn't you start with that?"

"Because it's not what you think." Giving up on the possibility of sneaking another minute of sleep, I sat up in Kevin's spare bed. "Kevin slept in his bed while I slept in the spare room. There was no intimate dinner, no casual conversation, no pillow talk and definitely no wild, clothes-ripping, moan-inducing sex."

"Bummer." She huffed on the phone, and I mirrored the sentiment.

"So what are you gonna do now?"

When Felix jumped back on the bed, I climbed from beneath the covers, staring at my sundress bunched on the floor. "First thing I'm going to do is get some new clothes." I'd slept in the only pair of underwear I had left, a delicate lacy set I'd donned just for Kevin, and would have to go out in my *date* dress from the night before in order to find new clothes for myself. The cat-calls that would incite definitely weren't fueling my desire to go shopping.

I'd just bent down to pick up my dress when a knock sounded a mere second before my door breezed open.

"Holy shit, Kevin," I squealed, dropping my phone to the floor as I covered up what was pretty much on full display.

"Oh, Elena, I'm sorry." Without even a lingering glance, he rushed back through the door he'd just entered.

What the fuck?

"Elena? Elena? Eleeeeennnnnaaaaaa?" I could hear Marilyn calling me from my phone, now lying next to my sundress.

Picking my phone back up, I muttered, "I've gotta go," and ended the call. I threw on my dress to chase after Kevin.

He sat at the kitchen table, his cheeks still glowing a bright shade of pink.

"Did you need something?" I asked.

He cleared his throat and answered, "I was just … I wanted to let you know I'd be leaving shortly and needed to lock up the house."

"Oh." I gritted my teeth. "Alright, well, let me just…" I was going to say brush my teeth, but my toothbrush was inside the apartment along with all of my makeup, my curling iron, everything. "Never mind. I'll just grab my purse and go."

"Thanks." He smiled and rushed out of the room.

I guess it was a good thing I wasn't dreaming about *him* last night, because it was exceedingly obvious that he had no interest in me, even after seeing my *goodies*. Once I'd grabbed my purse, I took a step out the front door to a blinding sun that sent me into a fit of sneezes. Was it possible someone could actually be allergic to the sun? If so, I definitely was.

Once my pupils had adjusted to the sunlight, I headed for my car and saw a staggering sight. There, leaning against my trunk, was the fireman from my dreams holding a bouquet of a dozen roses. No longer in his gear, he was dressed in a t-shirt pulled taut across the bulging muscles of his chest, a pair of cargo pants that hung at his hips and clung to those impressive thighs of his, and a pair of aviator glasses that I'd never seen look more sexy. I'd thought for sure I was awake, but seeing him propped against my car, there was just no way. After pinching myself and squirming, I realized that I was, in fact, conscious and continued toward my car.

"Hi," I breathed, biting my lip as I neared.

"Hey," he responded in a deep, husky voice. Holding out the bouquet to me, he asked, "How's your cat?"

As I took the flowers, I probed, "Are these for him?" It wasn't every day you met a guy who was a genuine cat person.

"Uh, no. For you." His blinding white smile had me pressing my legs together as I recalled what those teeth had done to my most sensitive places in my dreams.

"Oh, thank you." I smiled suspiciously. "But how'd you know I was here?"

"Chief said he overheard you talking to that guy about staying with him." He pushed off my car, moving infinitesimally closer. "I wanted to see how you were doing … wanted to make sure you were okay."

Really? I wondered briefly if he did this for every person who'd had a fire at their home. "I'm alright. Just need to go shopping for some new clothes and maybe — " I was cut off when Kevin came barreling out of the house.

"Elena," he panted. "You almost forgot your cat."

Was he for real? Why had he even offered to let me stay if he was going to kick me out on my ass the moment I woke up? I bustled to Kevin and took my cat, feeling highly perturbed. I wouldn't be able to get any shopping done with Felix around. If I spent any amount of time in any store, I'd return to baked feline.

"Great," I muttered as Kevin pulled away.

I returned to my car. The fireman's eyes roamed my body, lingering at my chest as my bodacious boulders bounced together. He visibly gulped before asking, "Problem?"

"Yeah." I sighed. "Gotta find a place to stow my cat so I can replenish my wardrobe." I carried Felix to my car, tossing him inside before rolling down the driver's window a crack.

"You wanna leave him at my place?"

"Are you serious?" Who was this guy? He was quite literally the stuff my dreams were made of. "I don't even know your name." *Although I called you all sorts of things in my dreams.*

"Oh, it's Justin." His hand reached for mine.

"Elena," I responded. When I took his hand, a pulse surged through me, up my arm, straight into my chest then quickly descended downward. We stood like a pair of complete idiots, shaking hands while staring intently into each other's eyes. Shrugging off my moment of stupidity, I finally pulled my hand away.

"Well, Elena, how about we take Felix to my place, then I'll take you shopping?"

Somewhere in the back of my mind lived a voice telling me this guy was a complete stranger who could do unthinkable things to me, but every unthinkable thing I could imagine ended up with me tied to his bed, and I just couldn't say no. "Umm, okay," I finally responded. "But I don't know where you live." *Because I just found out your name.*

"Grab Felix, and you can ride with me."

I kept hearing this voice say *This is crazy* over and over, but looking into those sparkling golden eyes, I just didn't give a damn. Snatching Felix from the car, I followed Justin to his truck and let him drive me to god knows where.

CHAPTER FOUR

*W*e'd driven about a mile up the road when I finally broke the silence. "So, Justin, what do you do?" Oh my god, did I just ask that? *Idiot, idiot, idiot.*

With a light chuckle and a smirk, he gave me a sidelong glance, but didn't say a word.

"Sorry. I guess, I'm just ... well ... to be honest, I'm a little nervous, because I don't know you or anything about you other than you're a firefighter, and I keep hearing this voice that says I must be crazy, but for some reason I'm in your truck, willingly going to your house, and oh my god, I'm rambling." I slunk down into my seat as heat flamed my cheeks.

That smirk was back on Justin's face as he turned and winked at me. Holy shit, I was done. If his was the last face I ever saw, I definitely wouldn't complain.

My rambling ceased as he occasionally looked my way, but most of his attention was on the road, driving us away from civilization.

"Meow," Felix piped up. "Meow, meow, meow, meow." And he now carried the weight of the conversation. He'd stretched up and put his front paws on the dash, suddenly interested in where we were going. "Meow, meow, meow."

What the hell, cat? We took a sharp left turn, and Felix came flying toward me.

"Merwow," he squealed as he flopped into my lap.

"Where are you taking me?" I stammered, hoping Justin would finally say something.

"My place is right up here." He pointed toward a driveway on the right as his truck slowed.

"Hmm," I softly cooed as Felix jumped from my lap into the floorboard. I voiced one of the questions I'd yet to ask. "Do you live alone?"

With that smoldering, sidelong glance of his, he nodded and smiled. Continuing on, we rode down a bumpy drive, and my stomach was doing somersaults for all sorts of reasons. We were almost to his house. I was going to the home of a perfect stranger. Good lord this man was hot.

When the truck finally stopped in front of a moderate-sized cabin, I sat and stared, suddenly overcome with nervous energy. Yes, I was in the middle of a terrible dry spell. Yes, I was dying to get under this man. And oh yes, he was hotter than sin, but even knowing all that, I found myself stuck staring from the passenger seat of his truck.

Justin watched me as he rounded the truck. The heat and avarice in his stare made me look away, shrinking further into my seat, because I finally realized the danger. A man who was capable of that stare would surely fuck me, but good.

With my purse strapped on my shoulder, I swooped Felix up from the floorboard and pressed him against my chest while trying to protect my virtue … if I had any left. When Justin opened my door, his strong hand took mine and pulled me from the truck.

"Come on." That low rumble in his voice made my knees weak.

I held onto his hand as he led me inside, mostly because I feared my knees would give out at any minute. "Uh … where should I…" My words ran out when he turned and looked down at me. His feral gaze weighed on me so much that I nearly dropped Felix.

"What?" He shook his head.

I gulped down my apprehension. Through a giant lump in my throat, I squeaked, "Where should I put Felix?"

"Huh?" He ran a hand through his wayward sandy locks before he answered. "How about in here?" Hastily, he threw open a door in the hallway that led to a small half bath.

I deposited my purse just outside the door and stepped inside, checking for anything in the space that might be dangerous to my sweet baby before I set him down and locked him in.

Before I could shut him inside, Justin appeared with a bowl of water and a can of tuna. "In case he gets hungry." After he'd set down the sustenance, he closed the door, trapping my sweet Felix inside.

For a moment, I watched the door. Then Justin moved closer, his gaze on my lips as I squirmed under his stare. Suddenly, his lips plunged to mine, and he devoured me with a kiss. My knees began to tremble as his tongue dipped inside, tangling with mine then tracing along the roof of my mouth, sending a shiver through my entire body.

His hands fisted in my hair, giving a slight tug to angle my head so he could take the kiss deeper. A soft, whimpering moan slipped between my lips, and Justin's hands fell from my hair, grasping my thighs and easily lifting me off the floor. Without hesitation, I wrapped my legs around his waist, and he pressed me against the wall, forcing an impressive erection against my core.

His mouth moved to my neck, delighting my skin with his stubble as he traced rough kisses along my nerves. I sent an, "Oh god," up in answer. His arousal pushed against the delicate lace of my panties, demanding entrance.

Holding my full weight with one hand, he eased the other forward, slipping his fingers beneath the lace to circle my bud. I began moving in his arms, grinding against his waist, craving to feel him deep inside me. His deft fingers continued a torturous movement as he carried me down the hall.

All at once, his kisses stopped. "I've been dying to taste you," he rumbled before dropping — literally dropping — me onto the couch. Before my breasts were done bouncing, Justin rested on his knees in front of me.

"All of you," he growled, then slipped the fingers that had teased me into his mouth. "So good," he crooned before spreading my legs and beginning a tormenting assault of kisses. He started at my toes and moved deliciously up my legs. He was inching closer to the one place I yearned for him to be. I couldn't wait to feel him the way I had in my dreams. But before he reached my center, he switched legs and began that agonizing ascent again.

"Oh god!" I was breathless, squirming in his touch as his kisses became licks then nibbles. It had been so long since I'd even been touched that I thought I might cum just from those delicious little bites up my thigh. "Please," I begged when I could feel his hot breath next to my most sensitive flesh. "Please."

"Hold on, baby," he muttered, pulling my ass forward on the couch. With a wicked grin, he gave a tentative lick over my lace panties, leaving his mouth over my wettest place and breathing me in. When he sat back on his haunches, he was still smiling that evil smile. "I hope you're not fond of these," he teased, tugging at my only pair of panties.

"I—," I started to protest, but in an instant, he'd ripped them and pulled the remnants from beneath me, dropping them on the floor just out of sight.

Guess I'd be going commando for a while.

He slipped back under my dress and buried his head between my legs, giving a tentative lick.

"Oh god," I cried again as his tongue licked me from ass to bud.

"So, so good," I heard him mumble as his tongue continued to lap up my center. When he'd found that sensitive button, he sucked and tugged, searing every bit of blood in my veins. My entire body was on fire as his teeth slipped over that delicate flesh.

Licking my lips, I tried not to move, tried not to knock him from that tantalizing tempo, but I had no control. One hand grazed beneath my dress all the way to my voluptuous breast and pulled the lace cup down to uncover the hardened nub beneath. His thumb and forefinger began delectably rolling my nipple as he continued to suck and nip.

My eyes were closed, and my breathing was scarce as I felt his movements in every inch of my body. He'd set me on fire, and I was dying for this fireman to put me out. With my orgasm on the precipice, I moaned his name, and was instantly awarded with a calloused finger slowly gliding inside my sheath. As his finger moved in and out, in and out, I was done for. My orgasm swept through every inch of my body, gripping his finger as he continued to move. My dreams didn't hold a candle to the way this man worked me over.

I trembled beneath him as he licked up my center one last time and emerged from beneath my dress. "You taste so. Fucking. Good." His words were punctuated between breaths. There was a predatory look on his face as if he hadn't already claimed me as his prey. "I can't wait to make you cum again."

My lazy eyes shot wide at his comment. *Cum again?* All of my energy had been sapped from me. I didn't think I could do more than lay there when he lifted me up and pulled my sundress from my body. Looking down, I saw one nipple was still aching beneath the lace fabric while my other breast was on full display. With my dress discarded, Justin moved up my body, reaching for my bra. "I don't think we'll be needing this," he said as he decimated the fabric and tossed the now useless garment to the floor. He was two for two in the underwear department.

Somehow, I'd ended up completely naked while he still had every stitch of his clothing on. I wanted to complain, but when his hand fell on one breast and his mouth on the other, words completely escaped me. Heat built between my legs, and I knew I could obtain the energy to go again. My hands roamed in his hair as he sucked and teased my supple mounds. "I want you inside me," I whispered. "I need it."

Looking up at me from beneath his thick lashes, he smiled that cheeky grin and began kissing up my chest, across my collarbone and back to my neck, nibbling there when I tilted my head to grant him better access.

"I might explode if you don't fuck me soon." I hadn't meant to say it, but my entire body felt like it was plugged in to some out-of-control electrical source, and he was the stabilizer through it all.

"Don't worry, baby. After fucking you all last night in my dreams, I'm going to fuck you so good you won't be able to walk tomorrow."

My mouth fell open, and my breath stopped. Was this guy for real? I sure hoped so. Sitting slack-jawed, I watched as he finally pulled his shirt from his chest and, ohmigod, he was even more gorgeous than I'd dreamed. His broad shoulders angled to impressive biceps accented with popping veins that begged to be licked. My eyes followed those veins to the calloused hands that had already worked me over and were now unfastening the button on his cargo pants.

My gaze held in anticipation, waiting to see that rigid shaft underneath. Tauntingly slow, he lowered the zipper and my eyes followed the V of his abdomen down, down, down, until his zipper was open and his pants fell away.

With no boxers or briefs to tend to, his impressive length sprung out to me. On an apprehensive gulp, I stared, wondering if he actually planned on putting *that* inside of me. It'd been far too long since I'd had any sex at all and *this* was the first thing demanding entrance?

Out of nowhere, Justin procured a condom and effortlessly rolled it on. Clearly he'd done this before, but at the moment, I didn't care because my only thought was how fast I could get that cock inside me.

Bending over me, Justin slid his tip inside, musing, "You're so tight. God, it's so good," before he sank in deeper.

While I lay beneath him, I felt so greedy for wanting every single inch deeper inside me. I wrapped my legs around his waist, pressed my calves against his ass, and urged him on, demanding more. From that very first stroke my veins zinged with pleasure. When he pulled out, my pussy ached with his absence. It was crying out for more when he punched back into me, deep into my core. With every stroke, I felt him plunge further inside, building that delightful tension once again. His movements were long and languid, his breaths punctuated, just like mine.

As my eyes rolled back, reveling in the feel of having every single inch buried inside me, I felt his arms slip beneath my thighs and lift me off the couch. "What are you doing?" I asked, wrapping my arms around his neck.

"Just hold on," he answered, carrying me back down the hall where this had all started. As hot, lustful kisses rained down on my lips, he pressed me into the wall, continuing that calculated rhythm, in, out, in, out, before he carried us further on. When we reached a darkened bedroom, he laid me on a bed and quickened his pace. From the edge of his bed he continued, driving my arousal higher and higher until I could no longer breathe.

Every stroke shifted me closer to the precipice. Every moan made me ache deep inside. I was spiraling into chaos, falling over the edge, feeling that glorious length sliding in and out. He had completely consumed me. I climaxed like never before, trembling beneath him. After he'd shuddered into me once, twice, and then once more, he cried out my name in pure ecstasy.

What I'd assumed was the end of an absolutely incredible fucking turned out to be just the beginning of a wild, sex-crazed night.

CHAPTER FIVE

*B*efore morning, I'd licked every square inch of Justin's body, worshipping the man who'd brought me to climax more than a handful of times. I'd lost count, and all sense of comprehension, after orgasm number three. After little more than an hour of sleep, my phone woke me with its incessant chirping. Reaching for the bedside table, I grabbed my phone, hurrying to silence it before it woke Justin, but when I rolled over, I realized he was gone.

Completely convinced that the entire splendid night of sex was just another dream, I answered my phone with disappointment. "Hello?"

"You bitch. Why didn't you call me back?" Marilyn chided from her end of the line. Since when was she a morning person?

Sitting up, I looked around the room and realized I wasn't in my own bed, or Kevin's spare bed for that matter. Last night was most definitely not a dream. "I, uh ... I was busy."

Oh god was I busy.

"Doing what?"

Her judgmental tone prompted me to pull the sheet higher, timidly covering my body. "More like doing who," I muttered.

"No way," she scoffed. "You didn't." She was laughing now and for all the wrong reasons. "You didn't need that spell after all, then."

"Well," I started, wondering how to break the news that I hadn't actually slept with Kevin, but with a near perfect stranger.

"Well, what? Did you or did you not sleep with Kevin?"

"I didn't," I replied.

"But you said," she started, undoubtedly pausing to decipher what little information I'd given her. "If not Kevin, then who?"

"A fireman?" Was I asking her? Of course it was a fireman. Of that I was certain. Every other detail about this mysterious man was completely lost on me.

"A fireman? Really? Like from the fire at your apartment?"

"Yeah."

"But how? You stayed with Kevin after the fire so how did you end up with Mr. Fireman? Did you track him down at the station?" She sure had a lot of questions.

"Actually, no. He tracked me down."

"What? Ohmigod. That is so hot."

"Yeah," I replied, suddenly breathless. I could still feel his stubbly kisses caressing my neck and taste his sex-drenched skin on my tongue.

"So where are you now?" She wasn't letting up with the onslaught of questions.

Biting my lip, I reluctantly answered, "I'm at his place."

"What? For real?" She was mouth-breathing over the phone. "Wait, is he laying right next to you, listening to our conversation?" Mentally, I could see her waggling her eyebrows at me.

"No. He's not here." I looked around the room, spotting a navy t-shirt hanging over the footboard of the bed. Snatching it up, I inhaled its Justin scent, part citrus and part amber, before slipping it on to roam the house.

"Where is he?"

I tiptoed down the hall, flashbacks of being pressed against the walls flickering in my mind. I'd just entered the living room when I finally answered, "I don't know." I was walking around a stranger's house in his t-shirt and nothing else.

"Huh?" A few seconds passed in silence.

I chewed my cheek as I searched for a note, but didn't see any in sight. Peeking out the window, I noticed his truck was gone. Instantly, my mind wandered to thoughts of him being called away by some emergency. Without thinking, I mumbled, "I hope he's okay."

"Whoa, Elena. You've spent one night with this guy, and you already sound like you've got it bad."

"I do not."

"You do so." She laughed. "So spill. What's he like?"

Wow. How did I answer that question? I barely knew anything about him. Trying to hide my ignorance, I stammered, "Well, he's tall ... built like a Greek god ... muscles that you just want to lick up and down."

"Uh huh."

"And his legs. Mmm. The sheer power in those tree trunks. Good lord."

"Okay, but what's he like?"

"Well," I bit my lip. "He's quiet, mysterious, sexy as hell."

"That's it? That's all you're giving me?" Her disappointment was palpable.

"Honestly, I really don't know more than that. He hasn't said much more to me than the fact that he lives alone and his name is Justin. Anything else was just uttered in the heat of passion. God, Marilyn, the way he fucked me felt like he was paying homage to me all night long."

"Hot damn, Elena, did he go in your apartment?"

"Well, yeah. He was one of the firefighters who went in after Felix." What did that matter, though?

"Do you know what this means? Do you realize?" She was in the midst of some *aha* moment, and I was completely confused.

"What, Marilyn? What are you getting at?"

"Elena," was the only thing she said.

"Marilyn," I retorted, completely annoyed.

"It's the spell, Elena. He's under the spell."

Gasping, I responded, "No." Holy hell, I'd just had the best sex of my life, and it was all because of some stupid spell. "There's no way." I chewed on that thought for a moment then said, "He doesn't even know me, Marilyn. It's not possible."

"With a spell, anything is possible."

"Fuck. What am I going to do?" I was panicking at the mere thought.

"Now hold on a minute. Just because you don't really know him doesn't mean this is all bad." She paused. "You said he was great in bed, right?"

"Well, yeah." Just the thought of what we'd done over and over last night brought a smile to my face. But he was a complete stranger and because of some stupid spell he was *in love with me?* "I think I'm going to be sick."

"Breathe, Elena. Just breathe." The sound of pages flipping echoed through the phone. "Look, if you're really freaked out, I think we can fix it. If you want to break the spell," she groaned and murmured on the line before she continued, "You just have to say *The love we formed while from a spell is something we must learn to quell.*"

"Really? Some stupid rhyme is just going to solve all my problems?" I rolled my eyes.

"Not all your problems, but this one? Yes." She sighed and added, "Say those words and whatever you feel for each other will completely disappear."

Feeling completely insane, I tried to remember the words, certain that if I screwed them up even the slightest bit, we'd end up in a bigger mess than we were now. "Can you tell me what to say again? I want to make sure I get it right." So I didn't end up turning one of us into a goat or unintentionally selling one of our souls to Hades.

"The love we formed while from a spell is something we must learn to quell."

"And that's it?" I may have had my doubts about the spell, but I was completely skeptical that a single sentence could fix whatever mess I'd gotten myself into.

"That's it."

I heard a truck rumbling up the drive and looked out to see Justin approaching.

"Crap, he's back. I have to go." I hung up the phone and raced back toward the bedroom, seeing Felix's paw poking from beneath the bathroom door as I passed. "Hey Fe," I whispered as I rushed on and climbed back between the sheets.

CHAPTER SIX

*G*ood morning, Elena," Justin purred as he entered the room in a white tank top and gray sweats that hung a little low on his waist. One hand carried a drink carrier with what I could only assume was coffee, and the other held a pink box that I hoped was full of sugary goodness. I was starved after last night's, and this morning's, festivities.

"Mmm," I moaned, feigning a slumbering state as I sat up beneath the sheets. In the seconds it took for him to get inside, I'd made no progress on deciding how or when to break the spell. In all honesty, my mind and my vagina were at odds. My mind said I needed to release Justin from the enchantment while my vagina was craving more of the best sex I'd ever had in my life.

As he flipped on the overhead light, his gravelly timbre crooned, "You're wearing my shirt."

Busted. "Yeah, I, uh ... I got cold," I lied. I just couldn't fathom walking around his house with absolutely nothing on.

"I can warm you up." He set the box and drink carrier down on the dresser, before inching closer with that wicked, savage look in his eyes.

He wasn't kidding when he said he could warm me up. Just that gaze had my heart rate kicking up a notch and my cheeks heating. But I needed to try and stay on track. "What's in the box?" I asked, trying to retain some of my cognition. With those sexy, come-hither stares, I was losing brain power by the second.

"Donuts." He picked the box back up from the dresser and brought it to me. "You like donuts, right?"

"Who doesn't like donuts?" I asked. Only crazy people would turn down a donut. All that sinfully sugary sweetness in a breakfast pastry? Yes, please.

Justin shrugged, setting the box on the nightstand next to my cell phone. "Sorry I left without saying anything. You just looked so incredibly peaceful laying there sleeping."

Heart melting. Sweetness overload. My mind was starting to give out and had granted all decision-making to my nether region. "Why didn't you come sleep with me?" I prodded. Seemed to me we both needed the energy reboot.

"Because the second I tried to lay next to you, I started watching the rise and fall of your chest and then I curled in next to you and felt your silky smooth thigh against mine, and all thoughts of sleep vanished. Leaving the house was the only sane thing I could do short of waking you and ravishing you again."

Good God, this man had a way with words … well, when he used them. After multiple orgasms in the last twelve hours, my vagina was already clenching out Morse code to call him back in again. "Are you tired now?" My voice had transformed from virtuous to voracious, and my hunger wasn't currently for those donuts on the nightstand.

"Baby, seeing you there in my t-shirt, sleep is the farthest thing from my mind."

I bit my lip as he slipped his tank top over his head revealing his magnanimous six-pack, then dropped his sweatpants to the floor. Just as before, his erection sprang to life from beneath his pants, and I found myself crawling closer, craving to lick that delectable shaft.

A feral growl rose from his chest as my hand gripped his incredible length and slowly slid from base to tip. I moved from the bed, falling to my knees before him, ready to devour him as he'd devoured me. I licked at the bit of pre-cum that had formed and took him into my mouth a little at a time. I let my lips brush over the head, easing down his length. Peeking at him through my lashes, I saw the *O* of his mouth and felt momentary pride knowing I was putting it there. After all the work he'd put in last night, I was going to make this count.

When he inched away from me the slightest bit, my arms wrapped around his thighs, and my hands clutched his ass, pulling him in closer, shoving that erection deeper in my mouth. I was moving over him, gliding back and forth, taking in his whole length as his moans grew louder.

"Holy fuck, where have you been all my life?" His hands fell to my head, holding on as I continued to suck and lick and taste.

I'd taken every last inch of him, rubbing my tongue along the base of his cock as it started to throb. Seconds later, his seed dripped down my throat in waves, sending a shiver of pleasure through me. When I finally set his cock free, I let out a wicked giggle and wiped my mouth like a good girl should, smiling up at him from my knees.

"Get on the bed," he growled, taking my hand as I stood from the floor, then shoving me back onto the sheets. "I'm going to make you cum until you can't breathe."

I gasped, as he climbed on top of me, straddling me as he ripped the shirt I was wearing straight up the middle. "That was *your* shirt." I said, thinking maybe he would've held more value for something of his own.

"Fucking thing never looked good on me anyway." And with that, his mouth came crashing down on my breasts, sucking and nipping; never spending too much time on one in the off chance that the other might get jealous.

"I want you inside me," I moaned.

Lifting his torso up, he looked down at me and countered, "Your wish is my command." Without hesitation, he donned a condom just before his back arched dipping his hips forward and meeting my precipice. Looming at my entrance for a moment, he took one hand to stroke my sweet bud just before entering my folds.

"Fuuuucccckkkkk," I cried, as my pussy wept in jubilation. That ache I hadn't noticed when I woke this morning was now being soothed by the caress of Justin's remarkable manhood.

With an animalistic groan, he uttered, "I just can't seem to get enough of you," surging into me with that delectable shaft. As he stroked my precious nub, his hips moved forward then back, hammering into me. My hands grazed up and down his back until my nails dug in, forcing him harder, deeper inside me. His movements transformed from long and fluid to quick and hungry bursts that had me seeing stars as he sent me closer and closer to the peak.

I was climbing higher and higher when his motions stalled and he took a long, hard look at me with those golden eyes. "What have you done to me?"

My breath halted. He drank me in, licking his swollen lips, then letting his teeth hold his bottom lip, but never took his eyes off of me. As I leaned up on my elbows, I greedily kissed him, pulling that bottom lip into my mouth and sucking as my sex clenched around him.

In a quick swoop, he lifted me from the bed, swiftly rolling me on top of him without breaking our contact. In one sudden turn, we'd gone from missionary to cowgirl, and now I was in charge.

My hips started slow, luxuriating in the intense way my body responded to him. There was a fullness deep in my belly and a clenching in my chest. My hips lifted as I glided to his tip before taking him back in to the hilt. Each time my legs vibrated from the hum I felt as I lifted then eased back onto him.

Justin gripped my waist and sat up from the bed, pulling me hard against his chest. Our sweat-slicked skin slid together as he leaned forward to sink his teeth into the curve of my neck. I lost all control and my head lulled back, reveling in the pain and pleasure.

I didn't think I could take anymore when his expert hand returned to those skilled circles he provided to my sensitive bead. As his fingers caressed and teased, my rhythm grew more urgent, craving that delicious friction. My movements were needier, more intense, as his fingers sent me higher. I hung onto him for dear life as I shot over that peak and tumbled down the other side. Moments later, Justin pumped into me with vigor, then once more before crumbling on top of me.

Out of breath and out of my mind, I made a decision. A spell may have bound us together, but I wouldn't let anything tear us apart.

AUTHOR AVA LYNN WOOD

AVA LYNN WOOD is an insomniac who writes to calm the voices. When the voices get too loud, stories are formed. She was born and raised in Texas but got to Florida as quick as she could, enjoying the fresh sea air and summer storms. When she's not writing, Ava can be found chasing her children all over the county, snapping photos of any and everything, visiting one of her local theme parks, or just spending quality time with her family.

To find out more visit: www.avawood.net

If you enjoyed *BURNING LOVE*, check out *FORGETTING YESTERDAY*

Missy Shaw thought she had her life planned out perfectly; do well in school, take her basketball team to state, and get a free ride to college. Her life wasn't perfect, but it was constant. With her best friend Karley at her side, she could handle anything.

After the death of her mother, however, her dad had other plans. Moving Missy from everything she knew in Kansas to the great unknown created a new set of problems. Attending a new school, all she really wanted was to be invisible, but that simple feat proved difficult when she has a run-in with the school's basketball star, Adam Miller, on her very first day.

Adam Miller is every girls dream; charming, sweet, and gorgeous. And for some reason he's very interested in Missy. His attentiveness is unnerving as Missy does everything in her power to evade his interest. Living with secrets she's not willing to share, Missy works to push Adam away in order to keep her family safe. But will keeping secrets really keep her safe?

Available at Amazon.

Jingle Spells is a feel-good holiday collection of witch-themed tales, from a witch hunt at the winter solstice, to a Christmas dinner in danger of being ruined by an imp. Here you will find a sparkly pair of shoes holding one woman's destiny, and a magical, mystery-solving cup of latte. Meet a broken young woman unaware of the powers she possesses, and a teenage boy with the fate of the world on his shoulders.

Featuring short stories from veteran authors J. Laslie, Sidonia Rose, and Heather Marie Adkins, and introducing Sammi Cox, Brittany White, and K. Laslie. Sit back with a steaming mug, light up the fireplace, and enjoy these six tales of magic, mayhem, and love.

Solstice Flames by Jennifer Laslie
A Midwinter Manifestation by Sammi Cox
The Witch's Shoes by Sidonia Rose
Molly by Brittany White
Holiday Dreams by K. Laslie
The Witch's Brew by Heather Marie Adkins

Download *JINGLE SPELLS* in ebook format FREE at Amazon.

ABOUT CYBERWITCH PRESS

CyberWitch Press is a licensed LLC in the state of Kentucky. Owner Heather Adkins has been operating as a freelance ebook and print interior designer since July 2011.

Heather is an author from Louisville, Kentucky with nearly twenty published novels across the major platforms, as well as stories in numerous short story anthologies. She has been an active part of the indie publishing community since May 2011.

Her experiences joining other anthologies paved the way for *CyberWitch Press Short Fiction Anthologies*. *Jingle Spells* was the inaugural book for this series, and *A Midsummer Night's Sidhe* is its follow up. She hopes each anthology she publishes through CyberWitch Press will only be better.

To submit your own short story for future anthologies, visit the submissions page at cyberwitchpress.com.

CyberWitch Press welcomes any questions or feedback at cyberwitchpress@gmail.com.

Made in the USA
Columbia, SC
08 June 2020